PURRFECT SAINT

THE MYSTERIES OF MAX 21

NIC SAINT

PURRFECT SAINT

The Mysteries of Max 21

Copyright © 2020 by Nic Saint

Edited by Chereese Graves

www.nicsaint.com

Give feedback on the book at: info@nicsaint.com

facebook.com/nicsaintauthor
@nicsaintauthor

First Edition

Printed in the U.S.A

I was leisurely lounging on the freshly mowed lawn behind the house I like to call my home, allowing the sun to play about my noble visage, and letting my paws dangle where they might. Birds were twittering in a nearby tree, lawnmowers were humming in the distance, and it was fair to say that this was a particularly wonderful time to be alive.

Next to me, Dooley was positioned in the same idle stance, lying on his back with his eyes closed, producing soft snores and generally enjoying a peaceful slumber.

No doubt you will tell me that a beatific scene like this is rare in a town as infested with crime and mayhem as Hampton Cove but you would be wrong. Generally speaking ours is a peaceable community, and if in the past I've given you the impression of the opposite I do offer my sincere apologies. It's probably because when I regale you with my adventures and the happenings in my little nook of the world, like any storyteller worth his or her salt, I like to skip the boring parts and jump straight to the hot stuff. In between gruesome murders and spine-tingling crime, not much actually happens in Hampton Cove, which is why I tend to leave those interludes out of my chronicles.

And I'd just closed my eyes and was about to pay a visit to the land of dreams where no dogs exist and food is always aplenty, when a strange phenomenon attracted my attention.

"Pshhht!" said the rhododendron bush located to my immediate left.

I glanced over, intrigued. Rhododendrons are known in the close-knit community of shrubs and plants as the strong, silent type, in that they rarely, if ever, raise their voice.

"Pshhhht, Max!" the bush said, and I frowned. I may not be a stickler for formality but I like to have established relations with a bush before being placed on a first-name basis.

But then it occurred to me I had probably fallen asleep already and this entire scene was only playing in my head. A dream, so to speak, if a pretty mundane one.

So I simply closed my eyes again and decided to ignore these attempts to snag my attention. If next a rabbit jumped out from under the shrub and invited me to join him down his rabbit hole for a nice little visit to Wonderland, that was all right by me.

"Max! Over here!" said the bush, and once again I was compelled to glance over.

"Max, that bush is talking to you," said Dooley, who'd apparently joined my dream.

"It's all right," I said. "We're sharing a dream. Rhododendrons don't speak. At least not in real life."

"I know," said Dooley. "But its voice sounds surprisingly a lot like Brutus's."

"Max! Dooley! It's me—Brutus!" said the bush now, and I had to concede that Dooley had a point.

So it was with some reluctance that I heaved my lazy form from the smooth lawn and decided to see what was going on with my fellow cat. Dooley and I traipsed over to the bush in question and ducked behind it. Brutus, when we finally joined him, seemed both relieved and anxious.

"I'm in big trouble here, you guys," he said. "Big, big trouble!"

Brutus is often in big trouble. He's one of those butch cats, whose forceful personality tends to clash with other, more laid-back ones inhabiting our cozy hamlet. Brutus was born and raised in the big city, you see, and New York City cats, when they are repotted to the suburbs, sometimes have trouble adjusting to a more leisurely pace of life.

"Did you get into a fight again?" I asked, not attempting to hide a hint of disapproval.

"A fight?!" the big, black cat cried. "I never get into fights! I'm the most peace-loving cat around! And if anyone tells you different I'll knock his block off!"

I noticed he'd balled his paws into fists and was eyeing me with distinct menace in his eyes. As I indicated: once a big-city scrapper, always a big-city scrapper.

"Are you on the run from the police, Brutus?" asked Dooley, curious. "Or the Mafia?"

Odelia and Chase, our humans, had watched an action movie last night, where a man was on the run from the police—or the Mafia—and Dooley and I had been forced to watch along, as is usually the case. Only very rarely do we get control over the remote.

"Lower your voices, will you?" said Brutus, and led by example by lowering his. "If she catches us it's all over!"

"Who? The Black Mamba?" asked Dooley, his eyes widening excitedly. In the movie a woman named the Black Mamba had been behind all the trouble our heroes faced.

"Who?" asked Brutus, who had missed the movie.

"The Black Mamba. She can kill with one look!" said Dooley. "And if that doesn't do the trick she can squeeze you so hard between her thighs you simply choke and die!"

Brutus frowned, and was clearly thinking the same thing I was: why would anyone want to kill a person by squeezing them between her thighs? Then again, that's Hollywood for you. They think up the strangest and most convoluted plots.

"It's Harriet," he finally revealed. "She's been hounding me about this guru she found."

Dooley laughed, and Brutus gave him a dirty look.

"I'm sorry," said Dooley. "But you said 'hounded.'"

"So?"

"Harriet is a cat, Brutus, so how can she hound you? Cats don't hound cats. Only hounds hound cats. When they're not hounding other hounds, of course."

Brutus grunted something that made Dooley wipe the smile from his face, and said, "Trust me, once she starts in on you, you'll know what I mean."

"Harriet found a guru?" I asked. "You mean, by the side of the road?"

"Not exactly. He's set himself up in a big house in town, and more and more people have started to flock to him. When we visited him last night the place was swarming with people—and cats."

Dooley and I shared a look of confusion. "Now when you say 'guru,'" I said. "What do you mean, exactly?"

"What do you think I mean? Harriet found a guru and now she wants to convert me to this guru's church or cult, and hopefully every other cat she meets. But I don't want to join a church or cult, Max. I'm fine the way I am, cult-free."

"I think you better tell Odelia," I said. "If Harriet has joined a new cult, Odelia will want to know about it. What's the name of this guru?"

"Master Sharif," said Brutus, looking distinctly unhappy now, and I didn't wonder. When one's girlfriend starts dragging one to gurus in the middle of the night, one objects. One argues. And one hides in bushes and consults with one's friends.

"You have to watch out, Brutus," said Dooley. "Especially if this Master Sharif invites you to take position between her thighs. That's how it all started for Indiana Smith, the hero in last night's movie. Before he knew what was going on, he was flat as a pancake."

"Master Sharif is not a she but a he," said Brutus, "and his thighs don't look all that lethal to me. His tongue is a different story. That cat can talk your ear off."

"That cat?" I said. "You mean…"

Brutus nodded sadly. "Yes. Master Sharif is a feline, just like us."

2

---

*T*ex was glancing out the window of his office with unseeing eyes. A nice little garden the size of a postage stamp stretched out before him. It was his wife Marge's pride and joy, and normally he loved the sight of it. He often liked to sit on the small bench, to read a book when business was slow, or during his lunch hour. Lately, though, he hadn't felt any inclination to sit outside any more than he'd felt like relaxing with a good book.

Dark thoughts had been preying on his mind, and when that happens, any book, however well written, fails to grip.

Vesta had already gone home, and his last patient had been handed a prescription to treat the gumboil he was suffering from, but still there he was, staring out of windows and wallowing in misery.

Finally, he heaved a deep sigh, picked up his leather brief-case, and strode from his office. Pulling the front door closed with a satisfying click, he turned to assume his daily walk home when a loud yell of "Tex! Doctor Tex!" made him halt in his tracks.

A shiver ran down his spine, for he knew whom that

6

voice belonged to, and he had no desire to converse with this person whatsoever, for it was he who was the cause of his recent troubles.

But Tex Poole was essentially a kindly man, and not prone to rudeness, so he paused and watched Jaqlyn Jones look left and right, cross the street and make a beeline for him.

With some effort, Tex creased his face into a smile sufficiently polite to satisfy the most critical acquaintance, and pushed away the sudden hope a nice big bus would hit Jaqlyn as he crossed the street, or even a ten-ton truck.

Unfortunately buses or ten-ton trucks are rarely there when you need them, and Jaqlyn reached the other side of the street unscathed.

He was a suave and handsome man in his early thirties, with perfectly coiffed hair, immaculately cut polo shirt, and sporting those boyish good looks that make women swoon and men suppress a sudden urge to smack them on the head with a blunt object.

"Tex, am I glad to see you!" said Jaqlyn, showing no indication of harboring the kind of rancor and resentment that Tex was harboring towards him. "I wanted to invite you to our garden party next Saturday. You and Marge simply have to join us."

"Garden party?" asked Tex, that same stilted smile still plastered across his features. Normally he was a garrulous and jovial man who smiled easily and often, but lately a care-worn expression had supplanted his customary happy demeanor.

"Yeah, we actually wanted to do it the week we arrived, but you know how it is. Getting the house ready, setting up my office, soliciting patients, we kept postponing, and it was only last week that Francine reminded me three months have gone by since we came to Hampton Cove and we haven't even invited our new friends and neighbors yet!"

"Three months," said Tex, nodding. "Has it really only been that long?"

"Yeah, it seems much longer, doesn't it?"

"Much, much longer," said Tex. More like three years. Or thirty.

"Say, I just saw Mrs. Baumgartner. Didn't she use to be one of your patients?"

"She was." One of his most faithful patients, in fact. Once upon a time Ida Baumgartner couldn't be dislodged from his office with a wrecking ball.

"She's been having trouble walking lately. Pain in her left ankle. She told me you attributed it to a slight sprain— nothing to worry about. But just to be on the safe side I sent her to a radiologist. Turns out she had a hairline fracture of the tibia. So I had to put her in a cast." He grinned. "She wasn't happy about it, let me tell you, Tex. Ha ha ha."

"A fracture?" asked Tex, taken aback.

Jaqlyn shrugged. "Anyone could have missed it, Tex, so don't beat yourself up about it." He gave the older doctor a light slap on the back. "Francine mailed the invitations yesterday. So talk to your wife and RSVP us as soon as possible, will you?"

"Will do," said Tex automatically, his mind filled with thoughts of Ida Baumgartner's tibia and how he could have possibly missed that fracture.

"See you, buddy," said Jaqlyn chummily, and darted across the street again.

"Yeah," said Tex quietly. "See you."

And as he resumed his short trek home, he wondered if ten-ton truck drivers advertised their services in the *Hampton Cove Gazette*.

&.

*I*n her office at the *Gazette*, Odelia Poole was just finishing up an article on the capture by the Mexican police of well-known criminals Johnny Carew and Jerry Vale. If at that moment her father would have asked her to contract a ten-ton truck driver for the direct purpose of committing vehicular manslaughter on his colleague Jaqlyn Jones, she would have strongly advised him against this particular scheme. But since her father had merely entertained the thought and not actually acted upon it, she continued putting fingers to keyboard until her article had reached its happy conclusion.

Happy for Capital First Bank, the bank Johnny Carew and Jerry Vale had robbed, though perhaps not all that happy for the two bank robbers in question. The criminal element rarely enjoys being collared and thrown into the slammer.

A tap on the doorjamb made Odelia look up, and she perceived she'd been joined by her editor Dan Goory. The white-bearded man who to many looked like a contemporary of Methuselah, was smiling. "Hard at work as usual. Really, Odelia, you are a marvel."

"Just earning my weekly stipend," she said, and leaned back. "They finally caught Johnny Carew and Jerry Vale."

"The crooks who worked for your mother?"

She grimaced, as if a thumbtack had suddenly been introduced to her buttocks. She was a caring and loving young woman, and the thought that her mother had been duped by the two gangsters she'd so unselfishly taken under her wing still stung.

Marge Poole ran the local library, and in that capacity had accepted a request from Johnny and Jerry's parole officer to allow the two men to spend their community service in the library's employ. Instead of giving of their best to serve the community, though, they'd dug a tunnel to the neighboring Capital First Bank, and had burgled a number of safe-deposit boxes. Not exactly a nice way to repay their debt to society.

"I have a new job for you," said Dan now. "What do you know about Soul Science?"

"The name sounds familiar. I'm going to say... Silicon Valley startup?"

"Soul Science is not a startup but a new church. They've just set up shop in the old Excelsior building on Tavern Street. So I think it behooves us to pay them a visit and find out more. And when I say us of course I mean you. I tried to make an appointment, but they told me they're not talking to the media, so…"

"You want me to go in undercover and find out all there is to know about them?"

"Bingo," he said. "Oh, and you better bring your cats."

"My cats? Why?"

"The main man, the guru, if you will, apparently has a thing for cats. In fact he's crazy about the creatures. Which makes you the perfect man for the job. Or woman."

"Gotcha. My cats and I are happy to accept your mission, dear sir."

Dan rubbed his face. "Oh, and try to snap a couple of good shots of the leader, will you? On the Soul Science website there's an old picture, and his face kinda looks familiar."

"Mysterious."

"All good cults are."

"Would you call them a cult?"

"I would—unless you can convince me otherwise." He tapped the doorframe again. "I know you'll knock it out of the park, Odelia."

"We aim to please, sir," said Odelia and was rewarded with a cheerful beard waggle.

"*A* cat guru? Really?" I asked.

I'd frankly never heard of such a thing, and in the course of my lifetime I'd encountered and experienced many a strange phenomenon.

"Well, Master Sharif is more of a co-guru," said Brutus. "In that he shares guruing duties with his human, who goes by the name of Master Omar. Omar takes care of the humans, while Sharif takes care of their cats."

"Sounds like a solid business venture."

"Oh, sure. You should have seen the place last night. Plenty of folks coming to see Omar, and cats to see Sharif. Except for me, since I was just along for the ride. Like a tourist."

Dooley, who seemed disappointed that no thigh-squeezing was going on at Casa Omar/Sharif, now said, "So what does Harriet see in this guru? Is he very handsome?"

Brutus gave him a reproachful look. "Of course not. Master Sharif only handles cats' spiritual needs—no hanky-panky involved. If he'd have made so much as a pass at Harriet, I'd have knocked his block off, guru or no guru."

I would have told him he probably should stop knocking people's blocks off, as it often gives the wrong impression, but he clearly wasn't in the right frame of mind for a stern rebuke. So I merely said, "You still haven't told us why you're hiding in bushes pshhht'ing at innocent passersby." Or lyersby, as in our case.

He heaved a deep sigh, and his face sagged a little. "Like I said, Harriet wants to convert me. She wants me to become a member of Sharif's flock and she'll stop at nothing until I've declared my allegiance and become a Soul Science follower, too."

"Soul Science?"

"It's the name of Sharif's outfit."

"Has a nice ring to it," I said. "But they shouldn't try and push you to join up." I'm a big believer in allowing every cat to join any creed, religion or other aspiration they choose, as long as no coercion is involved. "Why don't I tell her to lay off?" I suggested now.

"Wouldn't do no good," said Brutus. "She'll probably try to convert you, too."

I smiled a complacent little smile. "Let her try."

"Oh, there you are," suddenly a voice spoke in our immediate rear, and the cat of the hour suddenly appeared in our midst. Harriet is a gorgeous white Persian, who has been making heads spin and hearts race in our feline community ever since she made her debut.

"Harriet!" said Brutus, suddenly nervous. "We were just— I was just—I was going—"

"Have you ever considered that you're more than a body with basic needs, Max?" Harriet asked, ignoring Brutus's inane babbling and directing a stern look at me.

I smiled my coolest smile. This was it. A first attempt to break down my defenses.

"I have not," I said. "In fact I like my body and my basic

needs just the way they are and I see no reason to change a single thing about them. Not one little thing."

She blinked, but was not deterred. "Eating, sleeping, the occasional bathroom visit... Is that really all you want out of life, Max? Surely there must be more?"

"I like to sleep," I said, "and eat and take the occasional bathroom break. So what?"

"Have you never felt a deep inner yearning for more? A deep-seated feeling that there's another dimension out there —a dimension you have yet to fully explore?"

"There is Dyno-Kat," I conceded.

"Dyno-what?"

"Dyno-Kat is a new brand of kibble, designed to blow your faithful furry friend's mind," I explained. "I asked Odelia to buy it for me but she hasn't gotten round to it yet."

She tsk-tsked and shook her head like a school teacher when a pupil gives the wrong answer. "Now, now, Max. I know for a fact that you have a soul."

"I have a soul?" I asked, surprised.

"I've seen glimpses of it over the years. Beneath that soft and pudgy exterior there lurks a spiritual heart."

"I very much doubt it."

"We all have a soul, only we rarely use it."

"I have soul," said Dooley, and broke into a boogie-woogie, shaking his hips and swishing his tail and generally dancing to a snatch of music only he could hear.

Harriet stared at him for a moment, then dismissed him with a flick of her paw. "You have to join me tonight for a meeting that will change your life, Max. I promise you that all the answers to all the questions you've ever asked yourself over the course of a lifetime will finally be revealed. You'll leave Master Sharif's presence a new cat."

"I don't want to be a new cat," I announced, and thought that should fix her.

"Oh, Max," she said with a smile. "That's what you think now, but wait till you've heard Master Sharif address you personally. You'll never be the same again."

"What if I want to be the same again?"

"Well, you don't."

"Yes, I do."

"No, you don't. Shanille is also coming, and so is Kingman. In fact I've invited the entire cat choir. So if you don't come you'll be the odd one out, and you don't want to be left behind while all of your friends are joining the movement, do you, Max?"

I hesitated. This was a pretty powerful argument. "Shanille and Kingman are going?"

"And so are you. And Dooley, of course," she said, giving our boogie-woogieing friend a quick sideways glance, as if he was nothing but a mere afterthought.

"Where am I going?" asked Dooley, interested.

"Tavern Street 56 at eight o'clock on the dot. Be there or be square," she said, and then swept out from under the rhododendron, displaying all the hallmarks of a busy cult recruiter about to spread her message of hope and eternal peace to other beneficiaries.

"See?!" cried Brutus. "This is exactly what I was trying to avoid! Now we're all in for it. Master Sharif is going to recruit our friends, and if we refuse to sign up we'll be left out!"

"Impossible," I said. "Shanille, for one, is a staunch Catholic and will never allow herself to become a member of some sketchy cult. And Kingman is too down-to-earth and pragmatic to get involved in anything wishy-washy." I gave Brutus a comforting pat on the back. "Don't you worry about a thing, my friend. I have the situation well in paw. Tonight we're going to expose Master Sharif for exactly what he is: a fraud and a shill. And we're going to free Harriet from his spiritual clutches."

For some reason Brutus didn't seem entirely convinced. I, on the other hand, was absolutely sanguine about my scheme. No cult was going to recruit me. And definitely not a cult led by a man named Omar and a cat named Sharif. Or my name wasn't Max.

4

*O*delia stepped out of the offices of the *Hampton Cove Gazette*, her mind already thinking up ways and means of worming her way into this Soul Science leader's good graces and extracting the kinds of confidences from him that can be turned into hard-hitting copy, when she almost bumped into her grandmother, hovering on the sidewalk.

"Oh, hey, Gran," she said. "Is everything all right?"

What had prompted this inquiry into her grandmother's well-being was the fact that the old lady with the pale blue eyes and the little white curls was staring at her intently, a slight smile playing about her lips.

Suddenly Gran held up her phone and directed it at her granddaughter. "Odelia Poole, reporter for the *Hampton Cove Gazette*. What, in your opinion, is the meaning of life?"

Odelia stared at the phone, and saw from the green light that it was actually filming.

"Um…" she said, her usual eloquence suddenly abandoning her.

"The meaning of life," Gran urged in her raspy voice. "What's it all about, huh?"

"I…" She opened and closed her mouth like a fish on dry land for a few moments.

"Okay, maybe let's start with an easier one. Tell me about happiness."

"Happiness," Odelia repeated, staring from her grandmother to the phone. She'd been on camera before, but not when being bombarded with these hardball questions.

"Yeah, what makes a person happy?" Gran prompted. "What makes *you* happy?"

"I guess… a good meal," she said. When Gran rolled her eyes, she knew this wasn't the answer her grandmother was looking for. "My family makes me happy," she tried again.

"Wrong answer. Next question. What kind of society do you wanna live in?"

"What kind of society would I like to live in," said Odelia, stalling for time. "Um, I guess a nice society?"

Gran turned off her phone. "You're not even trying!" she cried. "A *nice* society? What kind of a lame-ass answer is that? I expected more from you. Being a reporter and all."

"You ambushed me! I wasn't prepared!"

"That's exactly the point. I want straight answers. Honest answers."

"I don't get it," she said. "What's this all about? Why are you doing this?"

Gran pushed out her chest. "I've joined a cult, and this is part of the program."

"A cult!" said Odelia. "Not Soul Science!"

Gran gave her a look of suspicion. "What do you know about Soul Science?"

"Nothing," Odelia said quickly. If whoever ran Soul Science didn't want to talk to the media and if Gran was now part of the cult, she better not let on that she intended to join them in her capacity as an undercover reporter. "But I'm very interested," she added.

"Oh, sure," said Gran dubiously. "You're interested in joining my cult."

"It's not *your* cult, Gran. You can't hog a cult like you can hog a piece of pie."

"I can, too. I like this cult. I found it and I don't want you to come and spoil the fun. Now go away," she said, waving an impatient hand. "I have more people to interview and you're wasting my time." And with these words, she turned away and accosted the next person who happened to come along, shoving her phone in their face and announcing, "Rory Suds, pharmacist, what is the meaning of life?"

For a moment Rory got the same deer-in-the-headlights look as Odelia had only moments before and looked as if he might make a run for it. Instead, he stayed put, probably thinking that whatever her faults, Vesta Muffin was still a customer, and one must always humor a customer.

"Well, I like to think that helping one's fellow man is a big part of it," he finally said. "Specifically by providing a superior customer experience when people visit the Rory Suds Pharmacy on Downing Street—the best place for all your pharmaceutical needs."

Odelia, shaking her head, decided to follow her grandmother's advice and move right along. If anything, this cult seemed right up her alley. If its leaders made their followers sneak up on unsuspecting passersby and ask them a bunch of tough questions, he couldn't have hoped for a better follower than an actual reporter, who was used to sneaking up on people on the street and hurling tough-ass questions in their faces.

Tonight, she told herself, she was becoming a member of Soul Science—whether Gran liked it or not.

A honk from a car horn told her that her attention was

needed elsewhere and when she turned she saw that her boyfriend had driven up and was parking at the curb.

She got into the car and settled into the passenger seat as Chase Kingsley merged into traffic. She must have still possessed the remnants of her recent encounter, for he glanced over and said, "Everything all right, babe? You look like you've seen a ghost."

"Not a ghost, my grandmother," she corrected the cop. "She's gone and joined a cult."

"A cult," said Chase with a grin. "You mean she's going around hawking *Dianetics*?"

"Worse. She's asking people about the meaning of life, and happiness."

Chase winced. A tough cop, who'd transferred from the NYPD to the Hampton Cove police department, answering questions about happiness and the meaning of life had probably never been part of his police academy training. "Ouch," he said.

"And when I said my family makes me happy she told me 'Wrong answer!'"

"I'm sure it'll all blow over soon."

"I doubt it," said Odelia. "She seems very anxious to spread the word."

"Well, as long as she doesn't start squirting people with sarin gas or invite them to drink poisonous potions I guess there's nothing we can do about it."

"The trouble is, I'm also going to join up, and Gran might blow my cover."

The car momentarily swerved into the wrong lane and once Chase had corrected its course, he cried, "You're joining up, too!"

"I have to. Dan told me to."

She realized she wasn't telling her story as well as she could have, so she gave him the beat-by-beat version, starting with Dan entering her office and ending with Gran wanting to keep her cult all to herself. When she finished telling her tale, Chase was silent for a few moments, then said, with a resolute look on his face. "If you're joining this cult, so am I. I'm not going to have you put yourself in danger without backup, babe."

She gave him a warm look. "Would you do that for me?"

"In a heartbeat," he assured her.

"Well, that settles it. Tonight you and I are becoming the newest Soul Science recruits."

"What about your gran?"

"I'll just have to convince her I'm not a stooge for Dan but the real deal. We're going to be the cultiest of cult members, Chase. My editor and my readers are counting on me."

"So... what *is* the meaning of life?"

"I just heard a good one. The meaning of life is providing a superior customer experience."

For some reason Chase didn't look convinced.

Being in a cult was going to prove tougher than she thought.

---

5

*T*ex arrived home feeling both annoyed and defiant. If you've been the top doctor in your town for the past twenty-plus years, it's tough suddenly to have to tolerate a rival, and especially when that rival manages to steal half your patients in a matter of mere weeks. He'd been silently fuming the entire walk home and was still fuming when he entered the cozy little home he'd made with Marge.

One of the advantages of having a mate for life is that you're provided with a sympathetic ear for your gripes, and it was in Marge's ears that Tex now vowed to pour all of his reservations about his fellow physician.

To his satisfaction his wife was in the kitchen, engaged in the preparatory stages of dinner, and after he kissed her on the temple, he immediately launched into a few choice remarks on a government that frowns on the hiring of contract killers for the purposes of dispensing with annoying young doctors who think they can just swoop into your town and take over your business.

Marge, instead of listening and nodding from time to time and generally displaying the kind of understanding and supportive attitude a harried husband likes to see in a wife at times like these, suddenly asked, "What do you think the meaning of life is, Tex?"

Tex was momentarily taken aback. He'd just been grasping for a third synonym of 'jackass' and was forced to perform the mental equivalent of a screeching halt.

"The meaning of life?" he asked, directing a look at Marge of utter bewilderment. He noticed now, for the first time since he'd arrived home, that Marge had a sort of worried expression on her face. A deep frown that told him she was brooding on something.

She took a seat at the kitchen table. "I've been talking to Vesta."

Uh-oh, Tex thought. It was never a good idea for anyone to talk to Marge's mother, who, in his expert opinion, probably should have been admitted to Bellevue decades ago.

"She interviewed me, and asked me a lot of questions that really made me think. Her first question was about the meaning of life, and I've been thinking about it ever since."

"I'm sure she didn't mean anything by it," he said. "You know what your mother is like. She's one of those scatter-brained people you really shouldn't pay too much attention to. Next she'll ask you about the history and usefulness of the cuckoo clock, or the difference between a red ant and a black ant. Just another day for her."

"But all her questions were like that. What's the meaning of life? What is real happiness? How can we make this world a better place? What is the soul... All very profound and important topics. And the strange thing is that I couldn't formulate an answer to a single one of them. I was absolutely stumped. And I'm the town librarian!"

"I would be stumped if your mother asked me about the meaning of life. A trick question, if you ask me."

"Mh," said Marge, not convinced.

"One question I can answer is the third one. How to make the world a better place. By removing people like Jaqlyn Jones from it. Do you know he had the gall to invite us to the garden party he and his wife are throwing?"

"Oh, that's right. I forgot to tell you about that. I got the invitation yesterday. Jaqlyn's wife dropped it off personally."

"Did you tell her in no uncertain terms where she could stick her invitation?"

"I did. I told her we'd definitely be there." And after delivering this bombshell, she got up and walked out of the kitchen.

Tex stared after her disappearing form, his jaw dropping. "But, honey!" he said finally, and followed her into the living room.

But before he could say more, Marge had turned and said, "Haven't you ever wondered if there's more to life than getting married, having kids and buying a house, Tex? Well, I have. And I think I'll join my mother tonight when she visits Master Omar."

"Master who?" he asked, the conversation starting to prove a little challenging.

"Master Omar. Mom says he's the only person who's got all the answers, and I, for one, am dying to hear what he has to say." She gave him a hopeful smile. "Will you come, too, Tex? Please? I just know it'll be good for us. It'll give us something to talk about."

"We have plenty to talk about. Jaqlyn Jones, for one, gives us plenty of food for…"

But she was directing a look at him that told him he was on the wrong track. So instead of gibbering on about Jaqlyn Jones, instead he found himself nodding dumbly.

"Oh, Texie," said Marge, attaching herself to his arm and kneading it affectionately. "You won't regret this. Vesta says you can ask any question you like and Master Omar will surprise you with the profoundness of his response. So you can ask him whatever is on your mind. The meaning of life, the location of the soul. Absolutely anything."

A sudden thought had occurred to Tex. He still had no idea who this Omar person was, or why he suddenly featured so prominently in Vesta's life, but it was true that he was a man in search of profound answers. A seeker, so to speak. So he nodded slowly, and said, "You know? I think I have just the question to ask this Master Omar of yours."

Marge smiled. "See? We all have questions, and maybe the time has come to ask them."

In Tex's mind only one question stood out, though, burning hot in its intensity, and it was indeed one of those important questions that keep a man awake at night, tossing and turning. Namely how to get rid of a certain young doctor named Jaqlyn Jones.

6

*I*t was still a little while before we were expected to put in an appearance at Master Sharif's place, so I decided to take a nap, after fortifying myself by snacking on some of those fine kernels Odelia likes to supply us with in generous quantities.

And I'd just snapped up my first piece of chicken kibble when the kitchen door flew open and Gran breezed in. Her cheeks were flushed and her eyes wild, which gave me pause.

She reminded me of the heroine of some romantic movie, in a scene following the couple's first meeting, when the heroine joins up with her best friend to tell her all about her new beau.

And as Gran fastened her eyes on me, I had the sinking feeling she was going to single me out for the best friend part and start dishing on some Tom, Dick or Harry she just met who'd taken her breath away.

"Max! Just the person I was hoping to meet!" she tooted with satisfaction. She then directed her phone at me and asked, "So tell me. What is the meaning of life?"

I raised a whisker. "The meaning of life is having a

comfortable home, a loving human who fulfills your every need, and a flock of great friends to share your adventures with."

Gran grinned from ear to ear. "Love it! Next question! What is happiness for you?"

Dooley had stepped in through the pet flap and glanced up at Gran, drinking in the strange scene.

"Are you making a movie?" he asked.

"Shush, Dooley," said Gran. "This is important."

"Can I be in it? I could be Max's goofy sidekick. Every movie's hero needs a goofy sidekick and I can be that goofy sidekick."

"We're not making a movie, Dooley," I said. "Gran is simply asking me some of life's important questions and I'm giving her a piece of my mind for the edification of her audience."

Though one had to wonder who she was going to show this video to. After all, we spoke in an ancient language only felines share—and a few choice people like Gran, Odelia and Marge. If she was going to put this video on YouTube, as most humans are prone to do with videos they shoot on their phones, she'd have to add subtitles.

Gran had pointed the camera at Dooley, who blinked, clearly ready to take up the part of the goofy sidekick and do it justice. "So, Dooley. Tell me about the meaning of life."

"The meaning of life is spending time with your friends," he said cheerfully. "And to avoid going to the vet."

Gran was clearly extremely satisfied with this response, for her smile widened. "If you were in charge, what kind of world would you create?" she asked next.

"Well, I like the world just the way it is," I said, "so I guess I wouldn't change a thing."

"I would!" said Dooley. "I'd make sure I don't get sick, so I wouldn't have to go to the vet. Oh, and I'd like more cheese snacks. I love cheese snacks."

"So a better world would contain more cheese and less vets," said Gran with a chuckle.

"Yeah, that seems about right," said Dooley, nodding seriously. "Oh, and maybe no more bad people. I mean, I know that Odelia likes to catch them and write about them, and that she depends on us to help her catch them and write about them, but wouldn't it be nice if we all got along and humans behaved the way they should? I think I'd like that."

"Very deep, Dooley," said Gran. "How about you, Max? You still want to keep everything the way it is?"

"Well... I could probably go for a world with less dogs in it," I said.

"Ooh, that's a good one!" Dooley cried. "I should have said that. Can I change my answer, Gran?"

"You can make an addition to your previous answer," she allowed.

Dooley looked straight into the camera and said, annunciating clearly, "I want a world with less dogs—or better yet, no dogs at all."

"And no mice," I added.

"Or rats," Dooley said.

"Some dogs are fine, though," I said. I was thinking of Fifi, our neighbor's Yorkie, who by all accounts was a fine, upstanding dog and never gave us an ounce of trouble. Even Rufus, Marge and Tex's neighbors' sheepdog, was fun to be around: he never gave any indication of wanting to chase us up a tree, and was always kind and polite.

"Yeah, some dogs are okay," Dooley amended his earlier statement. "So they can stay."

"Well, a lot of dogs are nice," I said. In fact we'd met many a fine member of the canine community in the course of our adventures. So contrary to popular feline belief not all dogs are bad.

Dooley thought for a moment. "Okay," he finally said, "so how about, no more bad dogs—the kind that try to bite us?"

"Even some of those aren't all bad," I argued. "Some of them simply want to protect their human and get a little carried away in doing so."

"True," Dooley admitted. "So how about... all dogs can stay but they have to behave?"

"I like that," I said. It was a statement I could definitely live with.

"So how about mice or rats?" asked Dooley. "I'm sure there are nice mice or even rats. It would be sad to see them go."

"You're right, Dooley," I said. "We should be kind to all animals, not just the ones we like. So rats and mice can stay, too."

Gran, whose arm was clearly getting tired, growled, "Can you guys please make up your minds? Dogs. Yes or no?"

"Yes, but they have to behave," I said.

"How about veterinarians? You still want to get rid of those?"

Dooley hesitated. "I'm sure they're perfectly nice people when they're not harassing pets, but maybe they can be retrained?"

"Yeah, Vena could easily find herself another job," I said.

"She could be a people doctor instead," said Dooley. "People don't mind to be prodded or stabbed with needles or poked with a thermometer."

Gran smiled. "Wait till I show this video to Omar," she said. "He'll be over the moon."

"I hate to disappoint you, Gran," I said, "but I'm pretty sure your Omar won't be able to understand a word we just said."

"Oh, yes, he will," she said. "Master Omar understands every living creature—at least that's what I've heard. And so when he instructed me last night to go out and find new recruits, I immediately thought of you guys. Four new recruits is going to net me a lot of credit with Master Omar. It might even give me access to his much-vaunted inner circle."

And with these words, she walked out.

7

*T*ex was still ruminating on the odd conversation he'd had with Marge, when the front doorbell chimed its merry little tune. Since Marge had walked out the kitchen door to pay a visit to their daughter Odelia next door, he opened the door and was surprised to find a familiar figure standing on the mat.

Francine Jones was a strikingly handsome woman in her early thirties, with auburn hair tied in a messy bun, remarkable green eyes and a charming tip-tilted nose. And even though Tex knew he should probably extend the animosity he felt for the husband to the wife, he felt himself incapable of including Mrs. Jones in his one-man vendetta.

"Hi, Doctor Poole," said Francine, looking a little bashful. "Can I come in, please?"

So charming and disarming was her manner that Tex suddenly felt like a real jerk for ever having had the notion to start a nation-wide search for ten-ton truck drivers with a penchant for running down small-town doctors.

"Oh, sure," he said, stepping aside.

She deftly moved past him into the hallway and he

glanced left and right to ascertain whether her husband wasn't hiding in the bushes somewhere, ready with a camera and hoping to snap incriminating pictures of Tex folding another man's wife into his arms. Francine might have melted the hard shell that was Tex's heart, but that didn't mean she might not still be a spy or agent dispatched behind enemy lines to entrap and ensnare.

Tex led Francine into the sitting room, a part of the house they rarely used, and bade her to take a seat on one of the overstuffed chairs while he took up position on the couch. He assumed this surprise visit was related to the garden party she and her husband were hosting, and that in the next few moments she would ask him to man the drinks table, or provide a trifle for the raffle.

Francine looked uneasy, so he directed the trademark Tex Poole smile at her, a smile designed to instill trust and elicit confidences.

"You're probably wondering what I'm doing here, Doctor Poole," she began.

"Please, call me Tex," he said.

She took a deep breath. "Maybe I better start from the beginning."

"Always a good idea," he admitted.

"My husband is a doctor," she said.

"I knew that."

"I mean, he's my doctor, obviously."

He wondered about her conversational tactics. If she was working her way around to the drinks table or the raffle prizes she was taking a long detour.

"Obviously when one is married to a doctor, one considers him her doctor, too. Only I've recently started suffering from some worrying belly aches, and when Jaqlyn examined me he said it was simply gas, and nothing to worry about. I..." She gave Tex a slightly embarrassed look. "The thing is, Jaqlyn is a very proud man, Doctor Poo—Tex. He wouldn't like it if I got a second opinion. And it's not that I don't trust him or anything. He's a fine doctor. But... I know what gas in the tummy feels like, and these pains are sharp pains, and they worry me a great deal. So... could you..."

He held up his hand. "Say no more. You want me to have a look at your stomach, is that it?"

She nodded quickly. "I'm so sorry for dropping in on you like this. In your own home, I mean. It's just that... Jaqlyn wouldn't like it if I came to see you. So I couldn't very well drop by your office."

"It's fine," he said, though he wondered what kind of doctor would prohibit his wife from seeking out a second opinion. Then again, if Marge would suddenly decide to pay a visit to Jaqlyn and ask for a second opinion on some suspicious spot she'd discovered on her nose which Tex had assured her was absolutely benign he probably wouldn't like it either.

Following his instructions, Francine lifted her shirt and he proceeded to carefully examine her tummy, frowning all the while. After asking her a couple of pointed questions, he nodded. "I can't be one hundred percent sure, of course, but I suspect you have the beginnings of a stomach ulcer. I'd advise you to have a gastroscopy and await the results. If I'm right, there's nothing to worry about. With the proper treatment you'll be right as rain in no time."

Jackie lowered her shirt. "I don't understand, doctor. I watch my diet—how can I have an ulcer?"

"Do you fret a lot?" he asked, still employing the soothing bedside manner that had made him so popular with his patients.

She gave him a sheepish look. "Lately I have been under a lot of stress. What with moving to Hampton Cove and helping my husband set up a new doctor's office and trying to find work for myself. It hasn't been easy."

"What do you do for a living?"

"I'm a kindergarten teacher. But so far it would seem Hampton Cove has all the kindergarten teachers it needs, and so do all the neighboring towns. I've been helping Jaqlyn, of course, but really what I want is to go back to work. I love my job, and I miss it."

"Why did you move to Hampton Cove, if I may ask?" It was a question he'd asked himself incessantly ever since Jaqlyn had set up shop across the street and started poaching his patients.

"Oh, Jaqlyn felt he needed a change of pace," she said vaguely. "We want to have kids, you see, and Hampton Cove seems like a wonderful place to start a family."

"It is," he said. "And I hope you do."

She smiled. "You've been very kind, Tex. I know you must have felt a certain resentment when Jaqlyn opened an office so close to yours, and took over some of your patients."

"Of course not," he lied. "There are enough patients in Hampton Cove to support two doctors. Now do you want me to arrange an appointment for that gastroscopy?"

"Yes, please. I don't want to tell Jaqlyn just yet. Not until I know what's going on."

She got up and placed a delicate hand in Tex's. "Thank you so much, doctor. I can't tell you how worried I've been."

"Everything will be all right," he assured her, and led her out into the hallway and opened the front door for her.

She paused on the doorstep. "What is the best way to deal with stress, doctor? Honestly?"

"The best way, of course, is to tackle the underlying issue. If being out of a job is causing you stress, finding gainful employ will immediately give you relief."

She nodded slowly. "Tackle the issue," she said pensively. "Maybe I will do just that."

And with these words she gave him another grateful smile and quickly walked away. And as she turned down the street, he saw she was furtively glancing over her shoulder.

8

*J*aqlyn Jones heaved a contented sigh. He was glad now he'd had the good sense of adding a couch as part of his office furniture. Even though he wasn't Sigmund Freud and strictly speaking had no need for a couch, he'd still managed to convince Francine he needed one so he could take a nap in between some of his more trying patients.

One such patient was now reclining on the couch, where he'd just left her, after engaging in a thorough exploration of her frankly stunning physique.

"Are you sure your wife isn't going to walk in on us?" she asked for the third time.

"No, she won't," Jaqlyn assured her. "First off, she knows better than to disturb me when I'm with a patient, and secondly, I've locked the door." He gave every indication of being proud not only of having had the foresight of adding a couch but also a door lock.

"We shouldn't be doing this, Jaq," said his last patient of the day. "I feel guilty."

There wasn't actually anything wrong with Monica

Chanting, at least not to the extent that she needed daily visits to the doctor, but then Jaqlyn had never bothered figuring out a better way of organizing this illicit affair. Monica was the red-headed and long-legged wife of a landscaper, and when she'd come in for her first appointment had ended up in Jaqlyn's arms, preparatory to the kind of behavior no doctor should ever engage in with a patient. Both consenting adults, though, they'd decided they enjoyed this daily respite from married life, and had since been conducting a torrid affair.

"I think we have to tell them," said Monica now, bringing Jaqlyn up with a start and wiping the self-congratulatory smirk from his face.

"Tell who?" he asked, though he had a sneaking suspicion he knew exactly who she meant. This wasn't his first extra-marital affair, but he'd hoped it would be the first one where he didn't have to come up with a bunch of excuses of why he couldn't divorce his current spouse.

"Your wife and my husband, of course. They have a right to know."

"No, they don't," he said immediately.

"Look, I think we've established that we're meant to be together, Jaq," said Monica as she got up from the couch and started dressing. "You're not happy with Francine and I'm unhappy with Garvin. So why not break the news to them and get married?"

He could have given her plenty of reasons why he didn't want to divorce Francine, but he decided to refrain from bringing such a mundane and boring topic as money into the conversation. He was still enjoying the postcoital glow and didn't want to spoil the wonders it did for his complexion. So he merely said, "Let me think about it."

"Please do. Because I'm ready, Jaq. I'm ready to commit to you. All I need to know is: are you ready to commit to me?"

He took her into his arms again and gave her a wolfish grin. "Oh, you bet I am."

*M*onica finally having left, Jaq locked up his office and walked the few streets that separated him from the new home he and Francine had acquired. It had cost them a pretty penny, but when he caught sight of the lovely little villa he couldn't help but think it was all worth it. How quickly things had turned around. Six months ago he'd been in the depths of despair, and now look at what life had brought: a thriving office with tons of patients and a new life in the Hamptons. Not too shabby for a reformed addict.

He stepped through the little gate, admiring the nice white picket fence, and let himself in with his latchkey. And it was as he placed his coat on the rack that he heard the sound of four tires exploding with a loud bang and a sly little smile lit up his face.

Moments later, his front doorbell rang, and he opened the door. As expected, his next-door neighbor Barney Sowman stood before him, his face a nice beet red, eyes blazing, the veins at his temples pulsating. If he were Barney's doctor, which he wasn't, he would have advised him to have a lie down before he suffered a coronary. Instead, he said, "Oh, hello Barney. Nice day we're having. Wonderful weather for a little stroll in the woods."

"I've called the police, you scoundrel," said Barney in response, and held up a strange device that Jaqlyn immediately recognized. It was a steel plate with sharp spikes sticking out of it. Police departments used it at roadblocks and they were called tire shredders.

"You destroyed my tires! Ripped them to shreds!"

"I have absolutely no idea what you're talking about, Barney. Why would I destroy your tires?"

"Oh, don't you play dumb with me, Jaqlyn Jones," said Barney, shaking a meaty fist. "You put this thing where you knew I'd come driving past."

"Well, that's exactly the problem, Barney. You're not supposed to come driving past. That access road is private property—my private property, and you can't simply drive across another man's land like that. There are laws, you know."

"There are laws against slashing someone's tires!"

In the distance, a police siren made itself heard, and moments later a squad car parked at the curb and a heavyset man got out. As he walked up to them, Jaq saw that it was Hampton Cove's chief of police himself. Alec Lip.

"What seems to be the problem?" asked Chief Lip as he waddled up. He was a large man with russet sideburns, hooded eyes and bushy brows who looked like a well-fed balloon.

"This man put this thing on the road," said Barney, waving the steel contraption in the Chief's face. "He punctured all four of my tires in one go!"

The Chief took the contraption and studied it. "Is this true, sir?" he asked. "Did you put this spike strip on the road?"

"First off, there is no road," said Jaq. "This gentleman keeps driving across my property, even though I've told him many times he shouldn't. Secondly, no, of course I did not put this thing where he would drive over it."

"So how do you explain how it got there!" Barney cried.

"Calm down, Barney," said the Chief. "Yelling and screaming and getting all worked up is not going to do anyone any good."

"My best guess?" said Jaq. "Must have been neighborhood kids."

"Neighborhood kids," repeated the Chief in a skeptical tone of voice.

"We've got some real rascals roaming these streets, Chief. You should probably do something about it."

Chief Lip gave him a scrutinizing look. "So if I study this spike strip for fingerprints I won't find yours on it, is that what you're saying, Doctor Jones?"

"Yes, that's exactly what I'm saying."

The Chief directed a sad look at Jaq's neighbor. "Show me where it happened, Barn."

And as he and Barney Sowman walked off to inspect the damage, Jaq couldn't help but smile. Good thing he'd had the presence of mind to wear surgical gloves when he put that strip down. And even better that he'd bought them in Hampton Keys, paying in cash. Deciding that the matter didn't interest him any further, he closed the door.

He was surprised to find that his wife wasn't home yet. Probably gone shopping, he gathered, and spent the next half hour sending a series of saucy texts to Monica, making sure to use the secret cell phone he'd bought especially for the occasion.

9

*O*delia and Chase had arrived home, and I could immediately see that she had a big announcement to make. She had this excited look on her face she always gets when she has something interesting to share.

"Hey, you guys," she said, crouching down and tickling my chin. "How was your day?"

"Oh, just fine," I said, deciding not to tell her about Harriet and Gran's sudden immersion in the world of Soul Science. I had a feeling Gran would tell her all about it herself, and so would Harriet.

"Where are Harriet and Brutus?" she asked, glancing around. "There's something important I need to tell you."

"Harriet is spreading the word about her new cult," said Dooley, who is rarely as reticent as me, "and Brutus is probably still hiding in the bushes."

Odelia raised an inquisitive eyebrow. "Pray tell me all about it, Dooley."

And so Dooley told her all about it. Apart from a few mh-mhs and uh-huhs Odelia was suspiciously quiet, and only when Dooley had finished telling his tale, with some minor additions by yours truly, did she say, "Wow. So this Master Sharif takes care of cat recruitment while Master Omar does the humans?"

"That seems to be the division of labor at Soul Science GHQ," I agreed.

She nodded. "I was actually going to ask you guys to join me tonight at the Soul Science meeting, but Gran seems to have beaten me to it."

"She tricked us," I said. "She asked us a lot of questions, filming the whole thing on her phone, and then said Master Omar would be over the moon when he saw our responses, claiming he can talk to cats, too."

Odelia frowned at this. "I very much doubt that. I've never met anyone who can talk to cats, apart from the women in our family."

"Well, Gran seems to believe him, and she told us to be there tonight to find out more."

"So now we've been invited to Soul Science three times," said Dooley. "First by Harriet, then Gran, and now you. So who's going to get the credit and join the inner circle?"

"Inner circle?" asked Odelia. This clearly was news to her.

"Gran said that if she earned enough recruitment credits Master Omar would admit her into his inner circle, but if she has to share the credit, she might not make it," said Dooley.

"Oh, boy," said Odelia, and glanced up at Chase, who'd made himself a cup of tea and now handed a second cup to Odelia.

She got up from her crouch and gratefully took a sip. "Apparently Master Omar has an inner circle and Gran wants to be admitted."

"Don't tell me. You want to get in on it, too," said Chase with a grin.

"Of course I want in!" she said. "I can't write an article

about Soul Science without knowing all there is to know about the cult."

"Maybe you can pump your grandmother for information once she's a member of this inner circle?" Chase suggested.

"Doubtful. Gran would never divulge any information if she suspects I'm going to use it for an article."

"Well, I guess there's only one thing to do," said Chase.

"What's that?"

"Recruit as many new members as possible yourself, earn plenty of credits, and become a part of this inner circle."

"Are you going to join Soul Science, Chase?" asked Dooley.

After Odelia had graciously provided the necessary translation, he said, "I guess so. Anything for my baby."

"You have a baby?" asked Dooley, surprised.

"Odelia is Chase's baby," I said. "It's an endearment," I added when he continued to be mystified. I directed my attention to Chase. "So isn't Master Omar going to frown on a cop joining his operation? He might think you're a police spy infiltrating his cult."

"I hadn't thought about that," said Odelia, and conveyed my words to her boyfriend.

"I'll just have to convince him otherwise," said Chase. "And if I bring him a dozen new recruits, he'll see that my intentions are as pure as the driven snow."

"A cop and a reporter joining up," I said. "He's going to need a lot of convincing."

"And that's where you guys come in," said Odelia. "If it's true that Master Omar can talk to his cat, you'll have to convince Master Sharif that we're not spies, so he can convince Omar. And then all will be well."

"Most families visit the cinema on their night out," I said. "But we visit Soul Science. Now all we need is for Tex and Marge to join and this will truly be a family affair."

And as if summoned by my words, just then Tex and Marge came walking in from the backyard. They both looked grave—or at least Tex did.

"There's something we need to tell you guys," said Marge.

"Oh, nice!" said Dooley. "Another family meeting."

"Don't tell me you've decided to join Soul Science," said Chase, preempting Marge's next words.

She stared at the cop. "How did you know?"

"It's like a virus," said Chase. "These things tend to spread."

"Gran has also joined up," said Odelia. "And Chase and I are also going."

"And so are we!" said Dooley happily. "Though Odelia and Chase are not actually believers, and neither are we. We're just going along for the ride, because we're afraid to be left out, and Odelia has to go because her boss told her to, and Chase is going because she's his baby and he doesn't want her to go alone."

Odelia stared at her mother, a sheepish expression on her face.

"Too much information, Dooley!" I hissed.

"Did I say something wrong?" he asked, taken aback.

"Yeah, Odelia being an undercover spy for the newspaper is supposed to be a secret."

"Well, I don't care about your motives, really," said Marge finally. "I'm sure that if there's something to be discovered there you'll discover it, and so will we."

"So did Alec put you up to this?" asked Tex. "Are the police now actively investigating Soul Science?"

"Oh, no," said Chase. "I don't think Soul Science is on Alec's radar yet. It's just that I don't feel comfortable letting Odelia infiltrate the cult all by herself. Even undercover cops have backup and a handler who keeps tabs on them at all times."

"But you will keep an open mind, won't you, honey?" asked Marge. "You're not going in there with any preconceived notions?"

"Oh, I'm definitely going to keep an open mind," Odelia confirmed. "If there's something interesting to be found, I'll say so in my articles. But if I find that this Master Omar is a fraud and a con artist, I can't promise I won't expose him."

"Fair enough," said Marge, satisfied.

And so the die had been cast, so to speak, and everyone's position made perfectly clear. So when Gran barged in, holding up her phone and asking, "Will you look at this—all of my new recruits all gathered together! Say cheese to your new master!"

So we all said cheese, though not wholeheartedly. Especially Tex seemed to suppress the urge to say, "The meaning of happiness? A nationwide ban on mothers-in-law!"

And as Gran spoke a few words into her own phone, possibly for the purpose of earning even more credits with her master, Harriet and Brutus joined us.

"So have you guys made up your minds yet?" Harriet asked.

"Yes, we're going," I said reluctantly.

"In fact we're all going," Dooley clarified.

"Define all," said Harriet, casting us a curious glance.

"Odelia and Chase and Marge and Tex," said Dooley. "We're turning it into a family outing."

"Oh, wow," said Harriet, beaming. "That's going to net me a lot of credits with Master Sharif. He might even admit me to his inner circle."

"Now wait a minute, missy," said Gran. "These are my recruits and my credits."

"No way, Gran!" said Harriet. "I signed up Max and Dooley and Brutus. They're my recruits. That's three credits in the bank for me."

"No, I signed them up," said Gran. "I shot a video and they were so excited they couldn't wait to sign on the dotted line and become converts. My recruits, my credits."

"Well, for your information, I talked to them first," said Harriet. "Long before you entered the picture with your silly videos and your silly questions."

"Oh, you conniving little—"

"Now, now, children," said Marge. "There will be no squabbling in this family. You'll share those credits fair and square."

"But I recruited them!" said Harriet.

"It doesn't matter who recruited whom," said Marge. "What matters is that we're going on an adventure together as a family. A united family," she added, giving both Gran and Harriet a warning look.

And even though neither Harriet nor Gran seemed convinced about the need to unite as a family, they still kept their tongues. But when I glanced over mere moments later, I could see that Gran 'accidentally' stepped on Harriet's tail, at which point Harriet equally 'accidentally' scratched Gran's hand, causing the latter to yelp in pain.

"Looks like Gran and Harriet still have a lot to learn about the meaning of happiness," said Dooley.

10

*A*lec Lip stood watching the devastation with a look of consternation. It was safe to say that when the company that produced spike strips advertised their wares with the catchy slogan 'Stop 'em dead in their tracks' they hadn't been lying.

"Well, Barney, I'd say your tires are ready for the scrapheap."

"But who's going to pay for new ones, that's what I'd like to know," said Barney.

"Doesn't your insurance cover an eventuality like this?"

"As if! They'll probably call it force majeure and raise my premium."

"We better get you a tow truck. Doctor Jones is liable to accuse you of trespassing and have you arrested."

"Me arrested! He's the one that should be arrested!"

"My hands are tied, Barney. The man has the law on his side. This is his property, and you can't just ignore him and keep driving across."

"I never had any issues with the previous owners. And

now since doctor high and mighty moved in I'm supposed to drive half a mile to reach my own plot? It's not fair."

"I know, buddy. I know."

Barney's little plot of land, where he grew anything from potatoes to tomatoes and everything in between, was positioned right behind Jaqlyn's property, and there had always existed an unwritten agreement that Barney could use the strip of dirt road that was located between the two neighboring houses. Technically, though, the road, which really wasn't much of a road, was located on Jaqlyn's lot, and the moment he'd moved in and had watched in surprise how suddenly Barney's old Land Cruiser had come trundling past, he'd put his foot down and taken away Barney's right of free passage.

"I'm taking him to court," said Barney now.

"You can try," Alec said dubiously.

"You don't think I'll win?"

"I'm not a lawyer, Barney, so I can't give you any legal advice, but as far as I know you need to have these kinds of agreements, these easements, in writing."

"I just had a verbal agreement with the Parkers."

"Ask a lawyer. Maybe there's some loophole I don't know about." He patted the other man on the back and when he glanced over to the Jones place, saw that the curtains were moving. Jaqlyn was watching, and probably wondering what was taking them so long. "And you know what?" said Alec, who had a strongly developed sense of justice, "I'm going to have this spike strip examined for fingerprints. I doubt whether Jaqlyn will have been so careless but you never know. And I'm also going to try and find out where this thing was purchased. With any luck I'll be able to prove that he bought it. Then at least we can make him pay for the damage to your car."

"Thanks, Alec," said Barney gratefully. "You're a real pal."

Alec called the towing company, and moments later they watched as Barney's car was towed away en route to the garage. Four new tires was going to set him back a nice chunk of dough, and even though Jaqlyn had the right to defend his rights as a homeowner, he didn't have to slash his neighbor's tires in the process. That was vindictiveness, plain and simple.

Alec's phone sang out a tune and he saw that his mother was trying to reach him. Picking up, he said, "Yeah, Ma."

"Alec, honey, I'm going out tonight and I want you to drive me," she said in surprisingly honeyed tones.

"Drive you where?" he asked, hoping it wasn't another one of those dance nights at the senior center, or, even worse, bingo.

"Oh, just some group I joined. Can you pick me up around seven-thirty?"

"Where is it?"

"Tavern Street."

"Sure, I'll drive you."

"And while you're at it, you might as well come in with me so I can introduce you to my friends. They're all dying to meet my handsome son the chief of police."

He rolled his eyes. He could already imagine what kind of group his mother had joined. Probably some knitting club of old ladies sitting around gossiping about their children and grandchildren.

"Sure, Ma, whatever you say."

He'd actually looked forward to a quiet evening at home, watching the game on TV and going to bed early. Then again, these shindigs never lasted long. He'd probably be home just in time to see the second half of the game.

He walked back to his car and heard his radio receiver crackle to life. He picked it up.

"Alec? Alec, where the hell are you?" Dolores's voice grated against his eardrum.

He grimaced and held the receiver away from the offended appendage.

"I'm here, Dolores. What is it?"

"There's been a number of reports of people being harassed on the street by some old lady with a phone asking them all kinds of weird questions. Apparently it's got something to do with this new cult that's set up shop in town."

"New cult? What new cult and what old lady?"

"I'm not sure, but from the description I get the impression it's your mom, Chief."

He groaned.

"From what I can gather," the precinct's dispatcher continued, "she's become the lead recruiter for that Soul Science cult, going around shooting videos of people, whether they like it or not, and asking them about the meaning of life."

"The meaning of life?"

"Yeah, and the meaning of happiness."

"Is that right?"

"You better get on top of this, Chief. I received a dozen complaints in the last hour alone. According to the last report that came in she's on Harrington Street right now."

"That's where she lives."

"I know."

"I'm on it," he said curtly, and clicked off.

So much for bingo night, he thought, and fired up the engine then peeled away from the curb, holding up his hand in greeting to Barney.

He reached Harrington Street in next to no time, and saw that Dolores hadn't been lying: there, on the sidewalk, his mother was holding up her phone and filming a couple of strangers and asking them a bunch of questions.

They didn't look happy and gesticulated wildly as they tried to extricate themselves from this impromptu street interview. As they walked away, she tried to push a flyer into their hands, which they promptly crumpled up into a ball and dropped in the gutter.

Alec got out and joined his mother.

"Did you see that?" she cried. "Littering is a punishable offense, you jerks!" she yelled after the couple.

"Ma, what do you think you're doing?" he asked.

"What does it look like I'm doing? I'm saving the planet."

"We've received a number of complaints—"

"Good! Someone should take this littering issue seriously. It's ruining our planet and we as a community should take a stand."

"Not about the littering. About you!"

"Me?" she said, giving him a look of such wide-eyed innocence she could have fooled him if not for his long association with the woman.

"Yes, Ma. You. You've been harassing people."

"Harassing! I'm simply asking them a couple of simple questions. They're free to answer or not. And I'm free to ask questions. This is still a free country, isn't it?"

"People don't like it when you shove a camera in their face and start filming."

"I don't 'shove' my camera in anyone's face. I merely record their responses, as I believe they're crucially important."

"And what's this I'm hearing about a cult? Did you really go and join this Soul Science nonsense?"

"It isn't nonsense. Besides, we're going tonight, so you can see for yourself."

He thunked his brow. "I should have known," he groaned.

"Should have known what?"

"That you'd try to trick me into doing something I don't wanna!"

"I didn't trick you into doing anything. I just asked you to drive me to my spiritual meeting, and while you're at it you might as well come in and introduce yourself to my new friends. They're all dying to meet you, and frankly I don't see what you're going all goggle-eyed over. Master Omar is a perfectly respectable man, and since he has all the answers to all the questions in the universe I don't see what there is to complain about. Don't you want to know the meaning of life and happiness? Well, then."

"No, I don't want to know about the meaning of life, or happiness, or whatever. I want you to stay home tonight and forget all about this Soul Science and this Master Omar."

A mutinous look stole over her face. "Are you ordering me to stay home?"

"No, I'm not ordering you to stay home—I'm asking you. For your own good."

"Well, I'm sorry but I'm not going to stay home while I have a chance to join the inner circle. I made so many recruits today that Omar is probably gonna wanna speak to me in private to give me his personal blessing. And you can't take that away from me, Alec!"

And with these words, she stalked off, leaving him shaking his head and tugging at the few remaining hairs that were left on his scalp.

And people asked him why he'd gone prematurely gray...

11

The time had finally arrived for the entire Poole family (and cats) to put in an appearance at Soul Science headquarters and clap eyes on the mysterious Masters Omar and Sharif.

Since Gran had insisted we arrive in style, she'd made sure the women were all dressed nicely, and so were the men. About us cats nobody bothered, as per usual. I guess I should probably have taken it as a compliment: cats are creatures so gorgeous we don't need to bother with unnecessary adornments like clothes, makeup or coiffures.

We arrived in two cars and had to park three blocks away, as all the parking spaces closer to Tavern Street had been taken.

"Busy night," Chase remarked as we got out. He'd been our designated driver, while Gran had her private chauffeur in the form of Uncle Alec, who'd grudgingly complied when she told him to comb his hair and put on a nice suit.

It appeared as if the last time he'd worn the suit was a couple of decades ago, as it smelled terribly of mothballs and lavender and was a little tight around the edges.

We all proceeded along the sidewalk, and soon were joined by many more people, all getting out of cars and heading in the same direction we were.

"Are they all going to the same place, Max?" asked Dooley.

"I guess we'll soon find out," I said.

"Of course they're all going to the same place," said Harriet. "There's only one show in town and that's Soul Science. Soon the entire town of Hampton Cove will declare itself Soul Science territory, and then the Hamptons, and then the rest of the country and the world. Can you imagine, you guys? We'll be able to tell our grandchildren that we were there when it all began!"

Her giddy excitement was infectious, and Dooley said, "Our grandchildren will be so proud!"

I could have spoiled the fun by pointing out that we were all neutered and spayed and so there were never going to be any grandchildren, but I decided not to. Harriet was right in that there was a certain electricity in the air. As if something new and exciting was about to happen, and I did feel uplifted by the general atmosphere of anticipation.

Even Chase seemed to feel it, for his eyes were shining as he gripped Odelia's hand a little tighter. The only one who wasn't impressed was Uncle Alec, but then apparently he'd had to endure Gran's incessant barrage of questions all through the drive for he now said, "Will you cut it out? I told you I don't want to know about the meaning of life."

"You're missing out big time, Alec," said Gran.

"I don't care!"

"Do you have a question for Master Omar, Tex?" asked Marge, who seemed as excited as the rest of the people making their way to the old Excelsior building, a known landmark.

"Oh, I have my question all right," said Tex, a grim expression on his face. "In fact I have *the* question."

"Good," she said. "This is our chance to find out the secrets of life so we shouldn't blow it."

Tex nodded seriously, as if to say that soon life would have no more secrets for him.

We'd arrived at the address indicated and found that it was a majestic house with a majestic entrance. The Excelsior building had been erected by a couple of billionaires around the turn of the century (the previous century, that is) and it looked majestic, its red-brick facade lit up by powerful halogen lights. Actual columns supported a portico and two guards stood sentry and gave every single person seeking entrance a once-over.

"No scanner?" asked Chase.

"Master Omar knows that no terrorists will try to gain access to his temple," Gran said in eulogizing tones. "They wouldn't dare."

"But how can he be sure?" asked Odelia, who clearly had trouble taming her reporter's instincts and bringing out the inner worshipper.

"Master Omar knows. He's like a god among men. And gods among men don't need scanners to keep the bad people out. They simply make sure that the thought of entering the premises doesn't even enter the thug's mind."

"Is Master Sharif also a god, Harriet?" asked Dooley.

"Of course he is," said Harriet. "Master Sharif is a god, and Master Omar is a god. They're both gods."

"But... how can a cat be a god?" asked Dooley.

"Cats have been gods before," she said. "In Egypt." Her eyes glittered excitedly as she threw her mind back to those long-lost times when cats were revered and worshipped as the next big thing. Yup. You had to hand it to those pharaohs. They treated us cats with the respect we deserve. "And now you better reserve your questions for Master Sharif," she said. "He'll be able to explain everything so much better than a mere mortal like me."

"Okay," said Dooley, and I could see that he was hatching a couple of doozies.

Finally it was our turn, and Tex cleared his throat and said, "The Family Poole. Ten strong."

The guard scrutinized us for a long moment, then gave the all-clear sign by jerking his thumb in the direction of the entrance and we all dutifully filed in.

Once inside, I was pleasantly surprised by the opulence on display there: marble floors, crystal chandeliers, column-supported ceilings. It all looked very airy and bright, and I immediately felt at home. Though as far as I could ascertain, no comfy couches were in evidence where a cat could curl up into a ball and snore the night away.

"Nice place," said Uncle Alec, sounding surprised.

"See?" said Gran. "I told you!"

"Told me what?"

"That Master Omar only settles for the best."

"Yeah, yeah, yeah."

People were milling about, sipping from flutes of something bubbly and effervescent, and talking softly. There were easily dozens of people there, maybe even more.

We all stood in a corner, glancing around, and waiting for whatever happened next.

"Masters Omar and Sharif usually hold their conferences in separate rooms," said Harriet in hushed and respectful tones. "Last night we were in a room on the second floor while Master Omar was on the ground floor."

"How many floors are there?" asked Brutus, glancing up at the ornate staircase, also marble, winding up to the next floor.

"I don't know," said Harriet. "I haven't seen the entire

house yet. But I've heard rumors that Master Omar has his private rooms on the top floor, where only members of his inner circle are allowed."

"An inner circle I'm joining tonight," said Gran.

"No, an inner circle I'm joining tonight," said Harriet.

Before the argument could spin out of control, a person appeared on the stairs and clapped her hands. "Master Omar is ready for you now. Will you all please join him in the main hall? And for our feline friends, Master Sharif is waiting upstairs."

"This is it, Max," said Dooley, clearly in the grip of the same kind of anticipatory excitement as the rest of the company. "We're going to learn all the secrets of life now!"

"Uh-huh," I said without much enthusiasm. I already knew all about the secrets of life: a good human and a nice couch to sleep on. Still, I was curious to meet this Master Sharif and find out what all the fuss was about.

So I followed Harriet as she made her way to the stairs, and then we were tripping up that cream-colored marble en route to the second floor and our first meeting with Sharif.

*O*delia watched with a touch of concern as her cats moved up the stairs. She told herself they'd be all right but still felt a little uneasy in her mind. Meanwhile, Gran was fussing over Uncle Alec, clearly unhappy with his general appearance and demeanor.

"Remember to be polite, Alec," Gran said.

"Yes, Ma," Uncle Alec grunted.

"And stand up straight. Don't slouch."

"I never slouch!"

"Yes, you do." She eyed her son critically. "And what happened to your hair?"

"What do you mean what happened to my hair?"

"It's gone."

"It's not gone."

"Yes, it is. Last time you had a nice big head of hair and now you're bald."

"I'm not bald. I have thin hair is all."

"You look like an old bald man. You look older than me."

"This is what I look like, Ma, whether you like it or not."

"How can I introduce you to my friends looking like this?"

"I don't care about your friends!"

"Maybe I'll ask Master Omar to give you hair. A man needs his hair."

"I have hair!"

"Not that I can see. I'll ask Omar to give you a nice hair transplant."

"Oh, God, Ma!"

"Exactly. Omar is a god, so he should be able to give you a nice hair transplant."

"No offense, babe," said Chase quietly, "but I think your grandmother has finally lost her last marble."

"I think she lost that marble a long time ago," Odelia whispered back.

They were shuffling in the direction of what appeared to be the main room of the house, where the conference with Master Omar was taking place. Chairs had been placed in a semi-circle around a large table, where several people were already seated.

"That's the inner circle," Gran commented. "Best seats in the house."

"You'll notice that all the seats are taken," said Uncle Alec.

"So? They'll just have to kick someone off the inner circle to make room for me."

"Ever the altruist," Tex grunted, earning himself a dark scowl from his mother-in-law.

They were directed to a couple of chairs in the back, near the wall, and Gran, clearly not happy with this seating arrangement, grumbled, "Last night I got seated in the first row. This is all your fault. I should never have recruited so many of you."

Finally they were seated and the waiting began. The room

was very airy and very bright, and there were cameras every-where, filming the entire thing.

"What's with all the cameras?" Odelia asked Gran, her resident expert on all things Soul Science.

"Oh, they have a YouTube channel," Gran said with a wave of her hand. "They post videos all the time. If you're lucky you'll be in one of them and become a minor Soul Science star."

"Are you in these videos?" she asked.

"Oh, sure. I'm in all of them."

"Why am I not surprised?" muttered Uncle Alec.

A sudden hush descended on the room, and when Odelia turned to look, she saw that a smallish man had entered. He was dressed in a plain knit sweater and looked like an accountant.

She looked away, thinking that surely he could never be the famous Master Omar, but then Gran gave her a prod in the ribs and loud-whispered, "It's him! Master Omar!"

Master Omar greeted the crowd with a kindly nod and took a seat at the head of the table. His hair was conserva-tively coiffed, and he had a square and doughy face.

"Huh," said Odelia's mom. "Is that Omar?"

"Shush!" said Gran. "He's about to speak!"

And so he was. "Friends, welcome to my humble abode," he said, in a surprisingly soft voice. "And I'm glad to see that so many of you have turned up. Let's start with a couple of questions." And then he turned the floor to those sitting at the table.

Odelia half expected them to ask about investment strate-gies and the difference between the debit and the credit column, but instead a young blond woman with a face like an angel said, "One of our members has singlehandedly brought no less than a dozen new people to our meeting, Master Omar. Not only that, but she's managed to convince her entire family to join us here tonight. Her name is Vesta Muffin, and surely she should be applauded for her fine work."

Suddenly all eyes turned to Gran, who had the decency to blush, and a polite smattering of applause broke out amongst those present.

"Indeed the force is strong in this one," said Master Omar. "Your spirit is commendable, Vesta. Please tell us, in your own words, how you managed such a remarkable feat."

Gran cleared her throat. "If you're inspired," she began, "it's easy for other people to get inspired, too. They sense the holy fire burning in your soul and it's infectious. Besides which, I told my kids that if they didn't join me I'd disinherit them, so there's that."

This elicited a smattering of laughter, and even Master Omar was shaking with mirth.

"Funny," said Chase.

"I wonder how my cats are doing," said Odelia. "I hope they're not too uncomfortable up there."

"I'll bet they're just fine," said Chase. "Besides, they've been in tougher situations than being cooped up with a minor feline deity."

"I can see that your family has many questions for us," said Master Omar. "Please go ahead and ask them and I'll do my best to answer them to their satisfaction."

Suddenly Dad shot up like a rocket, eager to ask the first question. But as he stood there, his brain working hard to formulate his opening remarks, suddenly a man strode in and took position next to Omar. He directed a slight smile at Odelia's dad, and the latter suddenly turned a nice and vivid crimson.

Odelia had no trouble following her father's thought process, for the man now flanking Omar was none other than... Jaqlyn Jones, who'd stolen half of his patients.

"Yes?" Omar prompted. "You had a question for me? Don't be shy. There are no stupid questions. Only stupid answers." He chuckled softly, clearly amused by his own joke.

"My name is Tex and I, um..." said Dad. "Um..." He seemed transfixed by the sight of Jaqlyn, then finally said, "What's... the meaning of life?" And promptly sat down again.

"A very good question," said Omar, nodding appreciatively. "And a very profound one." He turned to his left and said, "Jaqlyn. Do you want to do the honors?"

"Of course," said Jaqlyn. "In my humble opinion, the meaning of life is always to do right by your fellow man. To treat him with the respect he deserves. To love him like a brother. But I think Tex knows this already."

"Oh, you know Tex?" asked Omar, surprised.

"Oh, yeah. He's a doctor, just like me, and trying hard to take care of his patients. He doesn't always succeed, as he's only human, as we all are, but he does his best, and that's all that can be expected of anyone."

"Truer words were never spoken," said Omar. "Even doctors fail their patients from time to time, but they shouldn't let that deter them from keeping up the good work."

"Exactly. Because Tex knows that each time he fails a patient, I'm there to pick up the pieces," said Jaqlyn with a smile. "And that's the true meaning of life: to know that your friends have got your back and are there to help you up when you stumble and fall."

"Words to live by," Omar murmured.

Odelia could see that her dad's face had turned a dark shade of puce, and thought it best to change the topic before he burst forward and attached his hands to Jaqlyn's neck. So she got up and said, "I'm Vesta's granddaughter Odelia, and I'm so happy to be here tonight."

"As we are all happy you're here, Odelia," said Omar.

"So… can you tell us about the meaning of happiness?"

"Excellent question," said Omar. "Anyone care to answer?"

Dad snatched the microphone from his daughter's hands and said, in a tight voice, "Happiness is seeing a ten-ton truck thundering down your street and squashing—" Unfortunately some static momentarily intervened. "—horrible, no good—" More static. "—treacherous, deceitful, backstabbing —" And yet even more static. "—like a bug."

"Excellent, excellent," said Master Omar, nodding approvingly. He raised his hands. "Ask more questions, people. More questions. I'm here to answer them all."

In actual fact Odelia couldn't help but notice that Master Omar so far hadn't answered a single question. But then of course the night was still young.

An assistant tried to wrest the microphone from Dad's hand. Dad held on for a moment, his eyes still fixed on a smiling Jaqlyn, but finally let go and sat down.

"Well said, buddy," Uncle Alec whispered, patting his brother-in-law on the back.

$\mathcal{W}$e'd arrived on the second floor and found a lot of familiar faces in attendance. In fact it seemed as if every single cat in Hampton Cove had decided to show up at Master Sharif's little shindig.

"Is there a meeting of cat choir they didn't tell us about?" asked Dooley as he glanced around.

"I think Shanille has decided to organize an impromptu rehearsal," I said as I nodded to several of my friends. Shanille was there, of course, and so was Kingman, as Harriet had foreshadowed, but I also saw several others: Tom, Tigger, Misty, Shadow, Missy, Buster... Even Milo was there, our neighbor's cat.

"I have a bad feeling about this, Max," said Brutus. "They're probably going to wash our brains next."

"You mean brainwash us?"

"That's what I said."

"No, you said they're going to wash our brains."

"And they will!"

"I don't want my brains washed, Max," said Dooley, a

touch of panic in his eyes. "I like my brains just the way they are. Besides, I don't think brains are supposed to be washed. What if they get damaged in the wash? I need my brains, Max!"

"Nobody is going to try and wash your brains, Dooley," I said. "So just relax and take mental notes so we can tell Odelia exactly what's going on here."

He stared at me. "How do I take a mental note, Max?"

"Just... keep your eyes peeled."

"You want me to peel my eyes?" he asked, a horrified look stealing over his face.

"Just pay attention and try to remember what Sharif says." I smiled. "Use your brain."

The frown that appeared on his face indicated he was taking my words to heart, and he was already trying very hard to remember everything, even before it was said.

Contrary to meetings of cat choir, the cats present were all conspicuously quiet. And judging from the cold looks I was awarded, it was clear I was being entirely too loud. So I decided to keep my tongue and await further developments.

We'd taken a seat near the stairs, so we could beat a hasty retreat if needed, and as we watched on, suddenly a cat came striding in and took position on a small podium that had been erected especially for this occasion.

All the other cats sat quietly on the floor, and stared reverently at the newcomer, who was a petite gray cat with big hairy ears and a pointy nose. He looked like a big mouse.

"That's Master Sharif!" Harriet whispered.

"I gathered as much," I whispered back.

"Friends, I'm glad to see so many of you here tonight," said Master Sharif. "When we held our first meeting there were only five of us, and now look. Our numbers are increasing with leaps and bounds, and I can only salute our faithful and tireless recruiters. They're the ones who are making this miracle happen. They're the ones who deserve all the praise. So please can I have a round of applause for top recruiters Harriet and Shanille!"

The cats all put their paws together for a muted applause. It's tough to make noise when your paws are padded. Still, it was a sign of appreciation from the faithful.

I refrained from applauding, and so did Dooley and Brutus. The latter, however, quickly joined in when Harriet gave him a pointed look.

"Please tell us, Harriet and Shanille, how you managed such an amazing feat," said Sharif now.

Harriet and Shanille both got up at the same time and started speaking, then stopped, then started again, then stopped to glare at one another.

"I'll go first," said Shanille. "After all, I recruited most of those present here tonight."

"No, I recruited most of those present here tonight," said Harriet. "In fact I recruited you, remember, Shanille?"

"You did no such thing," said Shanille. "I recruited myself, and then I recruited the entire cat choir."

"No, I recruited cat choir," said Harriet, darting an icy look at the choir director.

"Ladies, please," said Sharif with a chuckle. "Let's all settle down. It doesn't really matter who recruited whom. What matters is that we are many, and now we can all go out and spread the word."

"And what is the word, Master Sharif?" asked a timid little cat reverently.

"The word is that it is time to put our soul front and center again," said Sharif. "As Master Omar teaches, it's not the material world that will grant us everlasting happiness but the soul, the center of our being, painfully neglected in the hustle and bustle of everyday life and the rush to accumulate as many material possessions as possible. The latest kibble, the newest cat toy, the best-smelling cat litter… But do these things give us fulfillment? Do they quench our inner thirst for peace and happiness? No, they don't!"

And as Master Sharif waffled on about the soul and cat litter, I quickly lost my interest. I was seated near the staircase, and as I darted a quick look in that direction, I wondered if anyone would notice if I simply slipped away.

And then I heard voices, and they weren't coming from downstairs, where the human contingent was gathered around Master Omar, same way the cats were gathered around Omar's pet, but from upstairs.

They say curiosity killed the cat, and it's true that cats are a lot more curious than humans. There's not a sound we can hear or a flicker of light we can see that won't attract our attention and induce us to go and explore further. So explore I now did.

While everyone was riveted by Sharif's railings against the newest brand of kibble, I snuck unseen up the stairs and went in search of the noises I was hearing.

I arrived on the third-floor landing and glanced around. The setup was much the same as one floor down, only here no gatherings of the faithful were taking place. A couple of couches had been placed, presumably for people to take a breather and contemplate their souls, and I could see that several doors led off the landing. One of those doors was ajar, and it was here that those mysterious voices were coming from.

So naturally I snuck in for a closer look and listen.

"But it's not fair!" a man's voice was saying. "Why can he sit at the master's elbow while I have to stay here and look at these stupid screens!"

"Yours is a very important job, Jason," said a female voice.

"Master has entrusted you with the task of ensuring security for His flock. You shouldn't question His decisions."

"But I don't want to be cooped up in here while Jaqlyn is down there with Him."

"Jaq is down there with Him because he doesn't have your particular set of skills."

"It's not fair. The Master promised me I could sit next to Him at the next meeting, and instead He asked that stupid Jaqlyn to sit next to Him. He took my place. Just took it!"

I shook my head. Whoever this Jason was, he sounded like a real crybaby, and already I was wondering if being close to the master had this infantilizing effect on all Soul Science participants. If that was the case it spelled trouble for the rest of us.

The voices had quieted down, and since there wasn't much more to learn, I decided to sneak back down again. I would have liked to take a peek inside those other rooms, one of which presumably was the inner circle's lair, but the doors were all closed.

With a slight sense of disappointment, I snuck back down the stairs again. When I arrived on the second floor, I resumed my position next to Dooley. He gave me a questioning look.

"I thought I heard something," I whispered.

"You didn't miss much," he whispered back. "He keeps going on and on about his soul. But I don't think he means soul as in soul music. But then what soul is he talking about?"

"I'll tell you all about it later," I said.

Harriet was scowling again. She seemed to have taken it upon herself to act as Master Sharif's enforcer, making sure all the participants were quiet and listening intently.

So we shut up and listened—though not nearly as intently as Harriet would have wished.

It was tough, as Sharif kept repeating the same message

over and over again, using different words: basically that there was more to life than kibble. I suppose he had a point. There is more to life than kibble. Wet food, for instance, or a nice slice of raw liver.

But somehow I got the impression that wasn't what he meant.

14

The evening was winding down, and still Master Omar hadn't said all that much. A few words addressing a topic that seemed near and dear to him: the importance of spending time getting to know one's soul.

"Imagine going on a leisurely stroll with your best friend," he said as everyone present hung on the man's every word. "You shoot the breeze, you have a great time, spending time with a person who gets you—who's always there for you. It's a great feeling, right?"

Murmurs of assent echoed through the room and Odelia stifled a yawn.

"You spend the day together, going for a walk along the beach, taking in some of that fresh ocean air, and when you arrive home you feel refreshed and invigorated, true?"

More murmurs of agreement and another yawn from Odelia followed by one from Chase. Then, in close order, Odelia's mom, dad, gran and uncle yawned, too.

She smiled. Apparently she'd started a yawn wave.

"Well, now imagine the same day, but minus the best friend. Just you walking along that same stretch of beach.

Only you're not alone, are you? You're in the company of your soul, and it's actually your soul that's your best friend. Your soul that has your back, and will never let you down. Your soul is your buddy, people, and don't you forget it. Now please repeat after me. All together now. My soul is my buddy."

"My soul is my buddy," all those present chanted.

"When you're feeling blue, just say 'My soul is my buddy.'"

"My soul is my buddy," said the chorus.

"When you're down and out?"

"My soul is my buddy."

"When life kicks you in the teeth?"

"My soul is my buddy!"

"Say it like you mean it!"

"MY SOUL IS MY BUDDY!"

"That's it! Now remember that!"

"Wow," said Gran. "That's really deep."

Odelia didn't think it was all that deep, but still murmured her approval of the master's words when he glanced in her direction.

"And now the moment you've all been waiting for," said Omar. "The announcement of this week's top recruiter. Drum roll, please."

Jaqlyn Jones made a drum roll sound, eliciting a groan from Odelia's dad, and Gran was already getting up, when Omar suddenly said, "Scarlett Canyon! Please join me at my table, Scarlett!"

"No way!" cried Gran, but her heart's cry was drowned out by the applause that rang out as Scarlett Canyon got up and sashayed from her seat on the opposite side of the room toward her master. Her flaming red hair was even more glossy than usual, under the bright lights that lit up the room, and her impressive bust more pronounced. Several men present momentarily forgot all about their souls and goggled as she walked past.

"Thank you, Omar," she purred as someone placed an extra chair and she took a seat.

"I want to file a complaint!" Gran said, her voice cutting through the noise.

All eyes turned to her, and Uncle Alec muttered, "And here we go."

"Oh, hi, Vesta," said Scarlett with a pinkie wave. "Hadn't seen you hiding back there."

"No way you're the top recruiter," said Vesta, her voice clear as a bell and her cheeks flushed with righteous indignation. "I'm the top recruiter. Omar said so himself at the beginning of the meeting."

"Master Omar praised you for bringing in your entire family," said Jaqlyn, speaking for his master. "He didn't mention anything about you being our top recruiter. Though your efforts are much appreciated, of course," he quickly added when Omar gave him a quick glance. "And we do hope you'll continue to bring in fresh recruits on a daily basis."

"I guess you'll just have to do better, Vesta," said Scarlett with a shrug.

"How can you tell people about the importance of the soul when you have no soul?!" Vesta demanded heatedly.

"We all have a soul, Vesta," said Omar. "And I have to say I admire your passion—your zeal! Now use that same zeal and passion to go out there tomorrow and bring many more people to Soul Science, and maybe next week you'll be the one sitting at my table."

"Yeah, try harder, Vesta," said Scarlett, and produced a tinkling little laugh that clearly had the effect of making Gran's blood boil.

"You know what?!" she said. "You can keep your table and your stupid inner circle! I quit!"

And with this surprising announcement, she stalked off, a white-haired volcano.

"Vesta!" said Jaqlyn, but Omar placed a hand on the doctor's arm and shook his head.

"What just happened?" asked Dad.

"I think Omar just lost his second-best top recruiter," said Uncle Alec with a grin.

The meeting pretty much was over after that mortifying scene, and as people got up and started chatting amongst themselves, Odelia grabbed Chase by the elbow and muscled her way through the crowd in an effort to reach Omar and ask him a couple of questions.

Unfortunately by the time she reached the table, the man was gone.

"Have you seen Omar?" she asked Jaqlyn, who was talking to Scarlett, his eyes thoroughly examining the woman's vertigo-inducing cleavage.

"Master Omar has retreated into his private chambers," said Jaqlyn dismissively. "He won't be coming out again tonight."

"But I need to talk to him," she said. "It's a matter of, um…"

"It's a soul emergency," said Chase, always a quick thinker.

"It will just have to wait," said Jaqlyn.

"Can't I have a private… audience?" asked Odelia.

Jaqlyn stuck his nose in the air. "Master Omar doesn't do private audiences. Master Omar only answers questions in his daily meetings with assembled worshippers. Why didn't you ask your question earlier when you had the chance?"

"It's… something I don't want to talk about in front of all these people," she said.

Jaqlyn scrutinized her for a moment, as if sizing her up, then finally said, "I'll see what I can do." And then he abruptly turned away again, to resume his perusal of Scarlett Canyon's assets.

"Nice try," said Chase as they walked away. "But no dice, I guess."

"Yeah, Omar is well protected. His lieutenant's main task seems to be to make sure he's not approached by his followers."

"What were you going to ask him?"

"Oh, this and that, you know. When he decided to start Soul Science. Where he got the idea from. That sort of thing."

"He probably got it from the back of a cereal box, like all good ideas," said Chase.

They'd joined Odelia's mom and dad and Alec again, and she noticed Dad couldn't stop glaring in the direction of his nemesis.

"Maybe you should just go over there and talk to the guy, Dad," she now suggested. "Clear the air, you know."

"I talk to him all the time," said Dad moodily. "He tells me what patients of mine he's been treating, and how happy they are that they finally found a doctor who knows his stuff, and I tell him 'Is that right?' and the next day we start all over again. The man never stops talking to me, or my patients."

"Maybe you should simply tell him how you feel," said Mom. "Tell him it's not right for him to steal your patients."

"You don't understand," said Dad, dragging a hand through his shock of white hair. "The man is as slippery as they come. Whatever you tell him, he always has some glib response ready to fire back at you. No, I'm starting to think the only course of action is to be advised of my rights."

"You mean legal action?" asked Uncle Alec.

Dad nodded. "There must be some law to stop a man from poaching a fellow doctor's patients, right? Something that can be done?"

"So weird," said Uncle Alec. "You're the second person

today who's threatening legal action against Jaqlyn Jones. The first was Barney Sowman, for slashing the tires of his car, and now you. The guy really knows how to rub people the wrong way."

"His wife dropped by the house today," said Dad, and Marge looked up at this.

"Francine Jones dropped by?"

"Yeah, she wasn't satisfied with the diagnosis her husband offered for the stomach pains she's been having. She was right. She probably has an ulcer and he simply dismissed her symptoms out of hand. The man isn't just a poacher of patients, he's a hack."

"Now, now, Tex," said Uncle Alec.

"No, he is. And I'm going to prove it." And with these words, he stomped off.

People stomping off was starting to become a recurring thing at Omar's event.

"Tex has been under a lot of pressure lately," said Mom apologetically.

"Has he lost a lot of patients?" asked Chase.

"I'd say he's lost about half of them, and more are canceling their appointments every day. They all seem to want Jaqlyn, and I don't understand why. Tex is such a wonderful doctor, and such a wonderful human being."

"With a wonderful soul," quipped Uncle Alec, earning him a reproachful look from his sister.

"It's causing him sleepless nights. But what can you do? People seem to love Jaqlyn, so he must be doing something right."

"Isn't this something for you, Odelia?" asked Uncle Alec. "Dig into Jaqlyn Jones and find out what's going on with the guy?"

"You think he's bad news?"

"Oh, I know he's bad news. But, like Tex said, he's as slippery as they come."

"I'll see what I can do," she said, inadvertently infringing Jaqlyn's copyright.

"Let's get out of here," Chase suggested.

"Where are the cats?" asked Mom.

"Our cats!" Odelia cried. She'd completely forgotten about them.

But it appeared as if the meeting upstairs had been concluded as well, for an entire feline contingent now came stepping down the stairs, meowing loudly amongst themselves.

And as her eyes met Max's, he winked. He'd discovered something, she just knew it.

We were driving home from the meeting, and to my surprise our humans weren't exactly brimming with the kind of good-natured bonhomie one would expect after spending the evening with an expert on the soul and the true meaning of happiness.

In fact they looked far from happy. As I gathered stirring things had taken place while they'd been in conference with the self-declared soul scientist. Gran had had a clash with Scarlett Canyon, her longtime nemesis, Tex had almost come to blows with Jaqlyn Jones, and Odelia had missed her window for an exclusive sit-down with Master Omar.

Next to me, a sullen Tex sat staring out the window, while Marge kept patting his arm in a bid to cheer him up.

In the front seat, Odelia was pensively gazing through the windshield, presumably thinking up schemes to get that Omar exclusive, while Chase was busy navigating Hampton Cove's streets, which were congested with other participants all attempting to get home.

Suddenly Odelia turned and asked, "I haven't asked you guys how things were with Master Sharif."

"A little boring," I said.

"Boring!" Harriet burst out. "Boring!"

"He kept prattling on about how material possessions are nothing but dross, and how the most important thing is the soul," I said. "So yes, I found the whole thing tedious. I happen to like my dross."

"God, you are *so* superficial, Max," said Harriet, shaking her head. "I can't believe I once thought you had depth. You have no depth at all. You are shallow. Shallow!"

"At least I'm honest about what I like and don't like," I said. "Whereas ninety-nine percent of the cats who were there tonight don't have a clue what a soul is."

"That's because they're new to Soul Science. They'll soon find out all about it."

"So it was all about the soul, was it?" asked Odelia, sounding slightly disappointed.

"I did manage to slip upstairs and overhear a private conversation," I said, and watched as her face lit up. Nothing to stir a reporter's blood like eavesdropping on a private conversation. If I'd said I'd witnessed some sensational scene of a highly private nature through a keyhole, she'd have yipped with joy. Unfortunately keyholes are not positioned at a comfortable height for cats to peek through. A minor design flaw.

So I related in a few words the conversation I had eavesdropped on, and Odelia turned contemplative, her reporter's mind whirring almost audibly. "Mh," she said finally. "Looks like Jaqlyn Jones is causing trouble and strife even at Soul Science headquarters. Did you happen to catch the person's name?"

"Jason," I said. "Apparently he works in security."

"I'll have to ask Gran," she said. "She might know who this Jason is."

I could tell from the resolute set of her mouth that she

planned to collar this Jason for an exclusive interview on the goings-on at Soul Science at his earliest convenience—or inconvenience. Nothing like a disgruntled employee or follower to dish the dirt on their guru. She would probably offer him a purse of gold in exchange for his life story.

"I think it was very rude of you to sneak out of Master Sharif's lecture like that, Max," said Harriet, who apparently hadn't had her fill of bickering tonight.

"I told you already. I was bored. And I heard voices. What is a cat to do?"

Brutus and Dooley both nodded sagely. They understood. A cat's got to do what a cat's got to do, and when voices sound where no voices are supposed to be, one follows one's instinct. And a good thing, too, as I had supplied my human with perhaps a vital clue to a story.

"Harriet?" asked Dooley after a moment.

"Mh?"

"What is a soul?"

Harriet directed a critical look at him. "If you have to ask, you're not ready to be told, Dooley."

"Ha!" I said.

Harriet looked up as if stung. "What's that supposed to mean?"

"You don't know what a soul is! Otherwise you would have told Dooley, instead of dismissing him with that feeble excuse."

"Of course I know what a soul is."

"Then what is it? Explain it for us noobs."

She pursed her lips, then said, "The soul is… Well, the soul is…" She swallowed uncomfortably, then finally cried, "Oh, I hate you, Max!" And lapsed into an offended silence.

"So what is the soul, Max?" asked Dooley.

"I have no idea, Dooley," I said. "But when I find out, you'll be the first to know."

"I think the soul is the eternal part in ourselves," said Marge now. "The part that's connected with the universe."

"You mean, like a miniature solar system in our belly?" asked Dooley.

Marge smiled indulgently. "Something like that, yes."

Dooley stared down at his belly, clearly wondering where all those stars and planets were located, exactly.

"I think a cat's soul is his personality," said Brutus, adding his two cents. "Like... I'm a happy-go-lucky cat, always sociable and kind. That's my soul. And Harriet here is sweet and bubbly. Max, of course, is a clever puss, and Dooley..." He glanced at Dooley. "Well, Dooley is Dooley," he said finally, which earned him a grateful smile from our friend, who was now massaging his belly, no doubt trying to locate his soul.

I wouldn't have described Brutus as happy-go-lucky, sociable or kind. More like a rough-around-the-edges reformed brute, but then of course that's just me.

Odelia sighed a wistful sigh. "If I ever manage to snag an exclusive with Omar, I'll be sure to ask him. All I know is that right now? My soul wants to have a good night's sleep."

I had no idea whether it was Odelia's soul that wanted to sleep, or some other part of her physical or psychological makeup. All I knew was that after having been induced to listen to Master Sharif for the past two hours, I absolutely concurred. I might not have understood what a soul was, exactly, or what Soul Science was all about, but it definitely was a wonderful cure for insomnia.

---

16

*T*ex was just getting ready for bed, still musing on that day's events, when suddenly the front doorbell rang. He directed a quizzical look at his wife, who was already in bed, thumbing through a copy of *Star Magazine*.

"Probably Odelia," Marge muttered distractedly. "Must have lost her key."

"She could have come in through the kitchen door," Tex grumbled. "Unless Vesta locked it again."

Dressed in his pajamas, he slipped his feet into his slippers and tripped down the stairs. And as he flung the door wide, fully expecting to find his daughter, he was not a little bit surprised when instead he found Jaqlyn Jones's grinning face staring back at him.

Immediately his mood, pretty foul to begin with, soured even further.

"What do you want?" he asked.

"Oh, hi, Tex. I'm so sorry for troubling you at this late hour," Jaqlyn caroled cheerfully, as if he and Tex were best buds on the eve of their annual fishing trip. "Look, I just wanted to clear the air. I don't know about you, but I felt a distinct tension between us at the Soul Science meeting, and I wanted to come over personally and tell you that I like you and I admire you and I have nothing against you whatsoever —on the contrary."

He stepped forward and Tex stepped back so Jaqlyn's tap, intended to land on Tex's chest, instead landed on his hand. Awkward.

"All I've wanted from the get-go is for us to be good friends and colleagues, Tex. So tell me, what do I have to do to earn your trust and, if possible, even your friendship?"

Tex thought about this for a moment. "Well, for starters you could begin by not poaching my patients," he said, deciding that he'd played coy long enough and the time had finally come to call a spade a spade and let the chips fall where they may.

"Poaching? Me?" Jaqlyn laughed. "Oh, Tex. Now I understand this odd animosity that seems to exist between us. Did you really think I've been poaching your patients?"

"You know you have. Dozens and dozens of them. I don't know how you do it, or what stories you tell them behind my back, but I've lost more than half of my regulars."

"Has it ever occurred to you that these people joined my roster simply because they wanted to, and not because of some insidious shenanigans on my part? I can assure you that every single one of my newly acquired patients has come to me of their own free will, and not because I've been badmouthing you. Just the opposite! I keep telling everyone how lucky they are to have such a fine and capable doctor at their disposal!"

"Then why do they all come to you?"

Jaqlyn screwed up his face in an expression of utter befuddlement, and drew his shoulders practically to his ears in an exaggerated shrug. "Beats me! All I can think is that people have this tendency to go for the new and shiny. You know how it goes. They may have a perfectly fine iPhone but still they want to buy the latest model. Or they have a great car and still they look at the latest introduction from a competing brand. Or they have a perfectly wonderful wife at home and still they can't help checking out that cute checkout girl at their local supermarket."

He gave Tex a conspiratorial little grin that Tex didn't reciprocate. He was one of those men who never checked out checkout girls, unless it was to ascertain whether that pimple on their nose wasn't skin cancer, in which case he gave them his card and told them to drop by his office at their earliest possible convenience.

He could see that Jaqlyn probably had a point, though. It was true that people often got tired of the old and trusted and yearned for something new and exciting. This was true for a lot of things, so why not for doctors?

Some of Tex's patients had been with him for so long that the arrival of a young new doctor in town probably worked on them like catnip: they simply had to have a nibble.

So he sighed and nodded. "You're probably right. It's probably a simple case of human psychology, just as you say."

"Of course it is! And I know this has been absolutely devastating for you, Tex. It can't be a lot of fun to lose half your patients to some hot young doctor moving in across the street, but I'm here to tell you that a solution is at hand."

Tex half expected Jaqlyn to suggest he was going to start refusing new patients. To draw up some sort of unwritten agreement whereby they divided Hampton Cove in different sectors, like Berlin at the end of WWII. Instead, Jaqlyn smiled widely, and said, "Next time I take a trip I'm going to refer all of my patients to you. And trust me, I take plenty of trips. In fact I've got one coming up next month. How about it, buddy? Deal?"

Tex suddenly felt very tired. "Sure, Jaqlyn," he said. "I'll handle your patients while you go on holiday."

He could have told Jaqlyn he was one of those doctors who very rarely took a holiday, because he didn't want to leave his patients in the lurch, but refrained from saying this.

"Thanks, buddy," said Jaqlyn, giving him that pat on the chest he'd been trying to land for a while now. "I knew I could count on you. I'm leaving on the sixteenth and I'm back on the Sunday." He turned to go, then remembered something. "Oh, you didn't hear this from me, but the Franklin Raiders asked me to handle their sports physicals this year."

Tex's jaw dropped. "The Raiders? But I always do their physicals!"

Jaqlyn gave him a helpless grimace. "What can I say, buddy? Shiny and new. See ya!"

And then he was gone, hurrying down the sidewalk to his shiny new Porsche, getting behind his shiny new wheel, and roaring off at full speed to his shiny new home.

As he closed the front door, Tex felt dazed. If Franklin High School was going to replace him, too, soon he wouldn't have any patients left.

"Who was it, honey?" Marge yelled from upstairs.

"Just a patient who needed some urgent advice!" he yelled back.

"You're way too nice, Tex!"

"I know," he said quietly.

He didn't want Marge to worry, but if this kept up he'd soon be out of a job.

And as he pounded up the stairs with heavy step, he thought that maybe the time had come to consider a radical solution to his problem. The kind of solution that would take care of the issue once and for all.

A resolute look came over him.

Desperate times called for desperate measures…

17

*V*esta had heard her son-in-law come stomping up the stairs and hoped that this time he'd stay put and let her sleep. That was the disadvantage of living under the same roof with your relatives: they kept getting in your way, occupying the bathroom just when you needed to go, leaving horrible hair in the sink, or dropping their shoes where you tripped over them.

Sometimes she wondered if men actually ever grew up or if they stayed the same infantile messy little boys all of their lives.

Long association with the opposite sex had convinced her the latter was true.

As she lay in bed, sleep unfortunately still wouldn't come. The stirring events of the evening had been too trying for a nervous system already a little taxed beyond its limits. Days of asking random strangers about the meaning of life and happiness and cajoling her family members into joining her newfound religious home had had that effect on her. Her initial fervor hadn't abated. Quite the opposite in fact. She felt even more fired up now than before, but what she couldn't abide was some scarlet harlot taking what was rightfully hers: the reward of being seated at the master's table.

It was just like Scarlett to ruin her big moment. Not only had the brazen hussy stolen Vesta's husband, and once upon a time even her job, she now deliberately had set out to steal Vesta's crowning achievement: becoming a member of Omar's inner circle.

And as these thoughts kept interfering with her desire to get a good night's rest, suddenly her phone chimed. She quickly grabbed it from the nightstand and frowned when she saw that some unknown joker desired speech with her.

For a moment she wavered. She got her fair share of surveys and robocalls and didn't need another loser trying to scam her out of her life's savings. Then again, what if it was important? What if it was the President of the United States wanting to offer her a seat on his board of advisors? Or an ambassadorship in the Bahamas or Monte Carlo?

So she picked with a growled, "What?"

"Vesta? Vesta Muffin?"

"You dialed my number, pal, so who do you think this is?"

"Please hold for Master Omar," the voice intoned, and Vesta gulped. Quickly she reached for her dentures, resting comfortably in a glass on the nightstand, and shoved them into her mouth. If she was going to have a midnight call with her guru she needed teeth.

"Vesta? Hi," Omar's quiet voice suddenly sounded in her ear.

"Master, what an honor," she said, and only now noticed she'd messed up by sticking her lower dentures where her uppers should go, and vice versa. She quickly rectified the situation, and said, "What can I do for you?"

"The situation between you and Scarlett has left me uneasy in my mind, Vesta," said Omar. "And I don't mind admitting I feel like this is all on me. I probably should have handled the situation better than I did."

Damn right he'd fumbled the ball, but instead she said, "Oh, no. This is all Scarlett's fault, Omar. She's one of those people who like to create trouble wherever they go."

"The thing is, Vesta, that I don't want to lose you. Soul Science needs you—I need you. So I wanted to ask you personally, is there any chance you'd reconsider quitting and stay on board instead? You're one of our top recruiters, as I already indicated during the meeting, and it's people like you that have made us what we are right now: the fastest-growing religion in the country."

"Well..." she said.

"Look, I'm not going to beat about the bush, or take up too much of your time, and I don't want you to decide right away. But will you at least sleep on it? You're very important to me, Vesta, and in case you were wondering, this is not something I tell all of my followers. You're special. I sensed it right away, and I feel it would be a huge loss if you quit now, both for us, and for you. So will you do me a favor and reconsider?"

"Oh, Omar," she said with a smile. "You had me at hi. You really did!"

"That's such a relief," he said with a chuckle, and she could hear he meant it. Such a great guy. "In Soul Science we talk a lot about the soul connection, and that's what I feel you and I have. A connection from soul to soul. You can feel it too, can't you?"

"Yes, I can," she said. "I felt it from the moment I laid eyes on you. A deep connection. In fact I haven't felt this strongly about anyone since my husband passed away."

"Well, that's fine then," said Omar. "Listen, if you're free tomorrow night..."

"Say no more," she said, suddenly feeling a little giggly. "I'll be there."

"Wear something special," he said warmly.

"Oh, you betcha."

After she'd disconnected, she was feeling as giddy as a schoolgirl after her first kiss. Did this actually just happen? Did Master Omar just ask her out on a date? Well, of course he had. The man clearly had taste, and saw the potential for a deeper association with one of his top followers.

And as she got out of bed and scampered to the window like a young gazelle, she leaned her elbows on the windowsill and looked up at the full moon with a tender smile.

Soon the wedding bells would ring out, and already she was practicing her 'I do.' It had been a long time since she'd been led down the aisle by her daddy, but she was ready to do it all over again, this time with the most deserving man in the universe. Of course her daddy wasn't amongst those present anymore to lead her down the aisle, but she could always ask Alec. Maybe Omar could even make her bald son's hair grow out again in time for the wedding, and make him look more or less presentable to give her away.

"Take that, Scarlett Canyon," she muttered under her breath, and as she heaved a happy sigh, she suddenly wondered if Omar would expect his bride to wear white. And if they'd get married in church. She'd have to have a word with Father Reilly, if he minded marrying the head of a rival church. But even if he did, she'd make him see the light, or else. No one was going to ruin what was surely going to be the best day of her life.

18

The next morning, bright and early, saw me and Dooley striding along the sidewalk, en route into town. We were on a mission from Odelia, who'd instructed us to find out as much as we possibly could about Master Omar and Jaqlyn Jones both. To the casual observer this might have looked like a tall order, but in actual fact Dooley and I are old paws at this detecting game. We have our spies and informants everywhere, and it was those spies and informants we were now going to pump for information.

Truth be told I'd also wanted to get out of the house as soon as possible, before Harriet woke up and launched into another discussion about the nature of the soul. Frankly I'd had enough religious discussions to last me a lifetime.

"Max?" now spoke Dooley. "Do you see anything different about me?"

I glanced over and told him that he looked exactly the same as usual.

He seemed to perk up at these words. "So you don't think my brain has been washed by Master Sharif?"

"As I told you last night, Dooley, brains can't be washed. A person can be brainwashed, but no actual washing of the brain takes place."

"Phew," he said. "I'm so relieved." This matter resolved to his satisfaction, he launched into a topic that clearly was close to his heart. "Do you think we'll have to go and listen to Master Sharif every night from now on?"

"I hope not," I said. "Frankly once was more than enough for me."

"For me, too," he intimated. "I was a little bored last night, Max. In fact I think I fell asleep at some point. I just hope I wasn't snoring. That would have been rude."

"It's all fine, Dooley. I'm sure Master Sharif is used to cats falling asleep on him."

We'd arrived in the heart of town, and lo and behold there was Grandma Muffin, holding up her phone and filming an unsuspecting bystander and asking him about the meaning of life and happiness.

"Odd," I said. "I thought Gran had quit Soul Science."

"She must have changed her mind," Dooley said as we watched on.

The innocent bystander was squirming, clearly unhappy about being caught on camera and asked a question he'd probably never in his life considered answering.

"The meaning of life…" he grumbled. "Um… the meaning of life…" He was an older gentleman with a walrus mustache and deep-set eyes that now flitted to and fro, clearly looking for the emergency exit.

"I'll put it another way. What makes you happy?" asked Gran.

The man brightened. Now this was a question he could answer with authority. "Garlic butter-basted steak, a bologna sandwich, a juicy quarter pounder with extra cheese—"

"No, I mean, what makes your soul happy," said Gran, smiling at her silly mistake. It's always important to use the exact verbiage when conducting these street interviews.

"My soul?" said the man, clearly surprised to discover that he had such a thing as a soul. "Well, um…"

"Don't listen to that woman," another voice piped up, and suddenly Scarlett Canyon entered the fray. She, too, was holding up her phone, and now told the man, "She's delusional—don't listen to her. Instead, answer me this: in what world do you want to live?"

"What world?" asked the man, his eyes darting from Gran to Scarlett and back. "What world?"

"Get lost, Scarlett," said Gran. "This is my recruit. Go and find your own."

"Clearly you're doing it all wrong," said Scarlett. "So let me show you how it's done."

"I don't want you to show me how it's done."

"I'm Soul Science's top recruiter for a reason, so let me teach you a few lessons on how to conduct the perfect survey."

"I don't need any lessons from you, Scarlett," said Gran. She was still holding up her phone, only now filming Scarlett instead of her intended victim, who stood eyeing the scene with pretty astonishment.

"Didn't you quit last night?" asked Scarlett, who was also holding up her phone, filming Gran. "I clearly heard you say the words 'I quit' and walk out, so what are you doing out here holding surveys? Are you trying to start a competing church? Cause if you are I'm telling Omar."

"For your information, Omar personally phoned me last night, and begged me to come back, so I told him I would."

Scarlett laughed a little laugh, throwing her head back as she did. "Of course he did! Really, Vesta, if you're going to lie through your dentures, at least make it sound plausible."

"Ask him. Ask Omar if he called me and told me Soul Science needs me and can't do without me. And ask him if he proposed to me in the process. He'll tell you."

"Proposed!" said Scarlett, her smile vanishing. "Omar proposed to you?"

"He asked me out on a date, but you know as well as I do that a proposal is only days away."

"Um... do you still need me?" asked the man whose soul apparently yearned to get away from these two squabbling septuagenarians.

"He asked you out on a date?"

"Yep. Just the two of us. And how could I say no? So you're looking at the future Mrs. Omar, and if I were you I'd show some respect, if you don't want me to tell my future husband to kick you out for gross insubordination to the First Lady of Soul Science."

Scarlett closed her mouth with a click. "Mh," she said.

"So I'll be going now," said the man, and started walking away.

"Not so fast!" Gran and Scarlett intoned simultaneously.

"But I have an urgent appointment!" said the man, and picked up some speed.

"Wait up!" Scarlett yelled.

"Yeah, the interview isn't over!" Gran cried.

They both were in hot pursuit now, the man skipping along the pavement, the two women close on his heels, phones out and yelling up a storm.

We watched the trio move out of sight, and Dooley said, "Is Gran really getting married to Master Omar, Max?"

"It would appear so," I said.

"But... does that mean Master Sharif is going to be our brother?"

I hadn't thought that far, but Dooley had a point. If Gran

married the Soul Science leader, Master Sharif would become part of the family.

Ugh.

19

*W*e decided to pay a visit to Kingman, Hampton Cove's unofficial feline mayor. As usual, the voluminous piebald was holding forth in front of his human's store on Main Street. He was basking in the sunshine, busily chatting up two young felines.

When he saw us coming, his face lit up.

"Max! Dooley!" he cried. "I wanna talk to you!"

The two felines were encouraged to move along, and Dooley and I took their spots.

"Listen," said Kingman, licking his lips and glancing left and right. "This Soul Science business. How much longer is this gonna be? Cause I gotta tell you I'm sick and tired of the whole thing."

"Um…" I said, slightly taken aback. Usually it's we who consult Kingman about such matters, and now that the roles were suddenly reversed, it took me a little while to adjust to my new position.

"Listen," Kingman said eagerly. "Ask Harriet. I mean, she's got the inside track, right? She's one of Sharif's top cats, am I right? So she knows what's what."

"Yeah, I guess Harriet is pretty involved," I agreed. "But frankly we're not exactly on speaking terms right now."

"Harriet doesn't think Max has enough soul," Dooley said. "And she doesn't like it that he's so fond of his dross."

"Eh?" said Kingman, mystified. He turned to me for an explanation, so I decided to give him one.

"Harriet feels I'm not spiritual enough," I said. "Too materialistic. I like my kibble and my naps and my creature comforts and she feels I should pay more attention to my soul."

"Who cares about your soul!" Kingman cried. "Can you eat a soul? No, you can't! So why should I care about a frickin' soul! Look, this has all gone way too far. Do you know that Shanille disbanded cat choir? She feels that spending time singing is not conducive to our spiritual growth, and instead we should all spend more time at Soul Science. Can you believe it?"

I said I could. Shanille appeared to have been infested with the Soul Science bug as badly as Harriet, or even more. Frankly I wondered what Father Reilly had to say about this, as his cat had effectively joined the competition. Then again, since Father Reilly couldn't talk to his cat the way Odelia could, he probably had no idea what she was up to.

"Look, we gotta fight back, you guys," said Kingman. "And it's not just me who's saying this. Plenty of cats have come up to me this morning telling me the exact same thing. They want this nonsense to stop, and life to go back to normal."

"I'm sure that in due course life will go back to normal," I said. "This is just a whim, Kingman. Before long the fascination will wear off and Shanille will open cat choir for business once more."

"I don't buy that," said Kingman, shaking his head. "I wish I could but I don't. No, sir. I think we need to take steps through the proper channels to make this thing go away."

"What do you suggest?" I asked, genuinely curious.

"I think we need to start a competing cult. One that's focused on the stuff that really makes us happy: a nice meal, cat choir, the company of friends." His eyes wandered to a couple of pretty felines passing by. They were giggling and batting their eyelashes. "The company of friends," he repeated, then shook himself. "Well, that's what I think."

"And who do you suggest will lead this competing cult?" I asked, intrigued.

In response he directed a pointed look at his own human, Wilbur Vickery, who sat behind his checkout counter, languidly ringing up groceries for one of his customers.

Wilbur Vickery is one of those people who look like a fossil, in that they appear to have died quite some time ago, but through some medical miracle are still walking among us. He is gaunt and stooped, with raggedy white facial hair, but his rheumy eyes still shine with a holy fire—the fire to fleece his customers for all they are worth.

"You want Wilbur to start a new cult?" I asked.

"Sure, why not? People like Wilbur. They respect him. They listen to him."

I doubted that. "But Wilbur is… old."

Kingman cocked a whisker. "Careful, Max. That's ageism. You gotta watch out for that kind of thing."

"That'll be thirty-nine ninety-nine," said Wilbur in his croaky voice.

The customer rooted through her purse, then said, annoyedly, "Oh, shoot. Looks like I left my wallet at home. Can I pay you tomorrow?"

"Read the sign, lady!" Wilbur said, pointing a crooked finger at a sign behind him that read, 'No Credit, No Way.'

'But—"

"Read the sign!"

"He sure is a people person," I said, though I very much

doubted whether a cult founded by Wilbur would draw a large crowd.

Suddenly another customer burst into the store, a harried look on his face. It was none other than Father Reilly, who manages the local branch of the Catholic Church.

"Can I leave these with you, Wilbur?" he asked, and unearthed a stack of flyers from a canvas shoulder bag.

"What's this?" asked Wilbur, none too friendly.

"Something I wrote last night," said Father Reilly.

"'Stop worshiping false gods,'" Wilbur read. "'Stop Soul Science before it's too late.'"

"We have to take action, Wilbur," said Father Reilly. "These people are taking over our town, brainwashing the good citizens of Hampton Cove. They have to be stopped now."

"I hear Vesta Muffin is one of 'em," said Wilbur, as he plucked his ratty white beard. I could see that the businessman in him was weighing his options: Vesta was a regular customer, and if he started boycotting Soul Science, she might start boycotting him.

"For crying out loud, Wilbur," said Father Reilly, raising his voice. "It's a damn cult!"

"Uh-huh," said Wilbur, still thinking hard.

"Their leader is a known blasphemer!"

"Is he now?"

"They're worshipping the golden calf!"

"You don't say."

"They took my cat and brainwashed her!"

At this, Wilbur looked up sharply. "They did what?"

"This Master Omar has a cat, called Master Sharif, and he's gathering all the cats of Hampton Cove and converting them to Soul Science."

"Pied piper," grumbled Wilbur, wriggling his bushy white brows with menace.

"Exactly! Soon all of our pets will walk out on us to join this cult!"

"Over my dead body!" said Wilbur, finally coming to a decision. He grabbed the stack of flyers from Father Reilly's hands and started handing them out to his customers. "Stop this petnapping cult now!" he said. "Read this ye and be warned!"

"See?" said Kingman with a note of triumph in his voice. "The fight against Soul Science has begun, and my own human is leading the charge!"

20

That evening, Marge was checking the fridge and wondering if it wouldn't be a great idea to get one of those newfangled fridges she'd heard so much about. The kind that know when you're running out of milk and eggs and automatically place an order with the store to have the items delivered to your doorstep. It would definitely be a great timesaver. She looked up when her mother walked in, looking resplendent in a pantsuit.

"What do you think?" asked Ma, twirling around.

"You look like Hillary Clinton," said Marge. Or the Queen of England.

The pantsuit was a bright mauve, and it hurt Marge's eyes to look at it.

"Yeah, yeah. But do I look like a preacher's wife, that's the question."

Marge raised an eyebrow. "You're going to be the wife of a preacher?"

"I'm still considering his proposal, but I'm leaning towards a definite yes," said Ma, looking pleased as punch.

Marge noticed she'd even put on makeup, and looked ten years... older, unfortunately.

"Ma, you really shouldn't use so much foundation," she said.

"I wanted to look like a blushing bride."

"You look more like the Corpse Bride. Here, let me fix you up."

They both retreated upstairs, where Marge proceeded to remove the thick layer of foundation from her mother's face with wet wipes and then applied makeup the way it should be applied.

"Haven't felt so nervous in years," Ma admitted. "I actually feel butterflies in the pit of my stomach. I haven't felt butterflies in the pit of my stomach since Jock Brownie tried to feel me up underneath the Franklin Raiders bleachers when I was fifteen."

Marge's face clouded. "Jaqlyn Jones dropped by late last night."

"Oh, was that who that was?"

"Yeah, he came to apologize to Tex, and extend the hand of friendship."

"'Well, that's a good thing, isn't it?"

"He also told him that the Franklin Raiders have decided to replace Tex with Jaqlyn for their sports physicals this year."

"Why?"

"Who knows why? It seems almost as if all of Hampton Cove is over Tex and embracing Jaqlyn as their new favorite doctor."

"Ungrateful bunch of fools," Ma grunted. "Tex is a wonderful doctor and a fine human being. Hampton Cove doesn't know how lucky they are to have him."

It was probably the first time that Marge had ever heard

her mother praise Tex, and it touched her heart—or maybe even her soul.

"Tex wasn't going to tell me, but I could see he was brooding on something, so I finally made him talk. And it's not just the Raiders either. Tex thinks that if this keeps up he'll be out of a job soon."

"And if he's out of a job, so am I," said Ma. "There must be something we can do."

"It's a free country. If people prefer Jaqlyn, there's nothing we can do about it."

"Let me talk to Jaqlyn. He's Omar's right-hand man, and with me soon becoming Mrs. Omar, I'm sure he'll pay attention when I talk to him."

"What are you going to say?"

"To lay off Tex's patients. He can tell them he's full up, can't he? He can tell them anything. Fifty-fifty seems like a good split between Tex and Jaqlyn."

"It's still a big loss of income. Fifty percent fewer patients means Tex loses half his income."

"We'll manage," said Ma, and patted her daughter's hand. "Nice work, honey. You were right. I did look like the Corpse Bride before."

"And now you look like a blushing bride," said Marge, satisfied with her work. "So you like Omar, huh?"

"Yeah, I think he's sweet. I mean, we haven't spent a lot of time together, but you saw him last night. He's a pretty impressive guy, right?"

"Yes, he's certainly impressive," Marge agreed. She'd come away from the meeting a little disappointed. She'd probably expected too much. Some kind of lightning bolt from the sky turning her life upside down and inside out. Instead it had been nice and kinda sedate. Interesting people and interesting conversations. Not exactly earth-shattering.

Still, Omar did seem like a nice guy, and if her mother liked him and he liked her…

"Do you want me to drive you?" she asked now.

"Nah. I'll drive. You better be here when Tex gets home from work. He'll need cheering up." She jumped down from the chair and smiled at her daughter, then gave her a hug. "Have I ever told you you're the best daughter a mother could ever hope to have?"

Marge choked up a little, and said, "And you're the best mom a girl could have, Ma."

"Thanks, honey." She took Marge's face between her hands. "Now don't you worry about a thing, you hear? I'm gonna fix this and we're all gonna be just fine."

"I love you, Ma."

"And I love you," said her mother, and darted down the stairs like a young foal.

🐾

*A*rriving at the Soul Science center, Vesta was in a cheerful mood. The day was still warm, as the sun was gradually setting behind the buildings, and as she locked the car and made her way to the Excelsior building, she was smiling to herself. She hadn't lied to Marge. She really was feeling those butterflies. She'd half expected Omar to call her to confirm their date, and maybe to suggest he pick her up, but then the guy had probably been busy all day talking to new converts and generally being a great church leader.

Probably tough to launch a new religion, especially since the field was so crowded already. Most religions had been around for a couple thousand years, with even the latest ones having cornered the market several decades ago. Then again, if anyone could do it, it was Omar. The guy had charisma up the wazoo, even though he looked like a man who might suggest at any moment to do your tax return. He had that *je-ne-sais-quoi* that made all the difference when picking a religious leader. Or your future husband.

She rang the front doorbell and to her surprise Scarlett Canyon came walking up the stairs behind her, dressed to the nines, which in her case meant her face was painted like a clown's and her dress had a hard time keeping her twin balloons from popping out.

"What are you doing here?" asked Vesta.

"Probably the same thing you're doing," said Scarlett with a smirk. "Omar called me and asked me to meet him here."

"That's impossible," said Vesta. "I'm meeting Omar."

"Well, looks like this is going to be one of those double dates. Or even a trio."

"Yuck," said Vesta disgustedly. "Why does everything always have to revolve around sex with you, Scarlett? Sex, sex, sex. Is that really all you can think about?"

"I never even mentioned sex! It's you that's oversexed, Vesta, with your dirty mind."

Vesta would have said more, for she had strong opinions on the subject and was eager to voice them, but the door opened and Jaqlyn Jones appeared. "Oh, there you are," he said a little dismissively. Then his eye caught Scarlett and a wolfish grin appeared on his handsome face. "Why, Miss Canyon. Do come in. Omar is expecting you."

Both Vesta and Scarlett walked in, elbowing each other as they muscled to move through the door first. And as Scarlett sped up to join Jaqlyn, linking her arm through his, Vesta's mood turned homicidal and she grabbed her rival's hair to yank her back.

"Will you... just let me..." Scarlett hissed, and tried to shove Vesta, who gave her a shove in return.

And both ladies were still engaged in a tug of war when they burst into the main room, and Vesta saw to her surprise that Omar was seated at the head of the table, along with his entire inner circle.

She gaped at the scene, taken aback.

Omar got up. "Ah, the ladies of the hour have arrived." He drew back a chair. "My dear Vesta. I've had my people wrangle us up a bigger table, just to make room for you. Will you take a seat? And you, of course, Scarlett."

Scarlett saw the look on Vesta's face and cackled with laughter. Vesta punched her on the arm and blurted out, "But I thought we had a date?"

"A date?" asked Omar, a look of confusion on his face. "What do you mean?"

Titters rose up amongst those present, and heat was rising up Vesta's neck, then seeping into her face. Soon she was blushing to the roots of her hair.

Jaqlyn grinned and said, "I think Vesta thought you asked her out on a date, Master."

Omar looked appalled, and that sealed the deal for Vesta. Stiffly, she said, "I'm afraid I'm going to have to politely decline, sir," and with as much of her dignity intact as possible, turned on her heel and strode out.

21

*O*delia had been trying all day to get a hold of the Jason Max had pinpointed as a possible weak link in the Soul Science machinery. Unfortunately the man was tough to track down. She'd asked Dan to call Soul Science in his official capacity as *Gazette* editor, and ask for an interview with Master Omar, then casually slip in a request to talk to any security people he might have in his employ, as he was writing an article about bodyguarding and wanted to have an insider's view, but the person on the other end had simply declined any requests for an interview and abruptly terminated communications.

She'd thought about clueing Gran in but had decided against it after being informed Gran had been proposed to by Soul Science's supposedly godlike leader.

No woman would ever dish on her future husband's private affairs, not even to please a loving granddaughter, so that avenue was closed, too.

So finally she'd decided to do things the old-fashioned way: she was going to stake out the Soul Science headquarters, take pictures of everyone going in and out and try to piece together a snapshot of its power structure.

And so it was that she was sitting in her car, across the street from Tavern Street 56, keeping a close eye on the goings-on at that auspicious address, when she became aware of a familiar face trudging up the steps to ring the front doorbell, immediately followed by a second familiar face: Gran and Scarlett Canyon.

She relaxed when she realized this was probably the date Mom had mentioned when relating Gran's shock wedding announcement. The only question was: what was Scarlett doing there? Unless she'd been earmarked as Gran's brides-maid, which wasn't likely.

Moments later, Gran came stepping out again, and judging from her expression no wedding bells were going to ring out any time soon.

So Odelia, against the unwritten rules of her guild, decided to break cover and rolled down her window.

"Gran!" she yelled. "Over here!"

Her grandmother eyed her a little dully at first, then, acknowledging her presence, shuffled over, not half as ener-getic and full of vim and pep as she had been upon arrival.

She got into the car and sank down onto the passenger seat. "If you've come here to gloat, don't bother. Scarlett's already done all the gloating I can stomach for one day."

"What happened?" she asked simply. She could see Gran was not in her usual can-do devil-may-care frame of mind.

"I made a big fool of myself, that's what happened," said the old lady, who was rocking a mauve pantsuit. "I went in there thinking I was going on a date with Omar, but instead he merely wanted me to join his inner circle."

"But I thought that's what you wanted?"

"Until last night, that's exactly what I wanted. But after

what I assumed was a proposal of marriage being offered a seat at the man's table suddenly doesn't cut it."

"I'm sorry, Gran," she said, taking her grandmother's hand and patting it consolingly.

Gran raised her eyes to Odelia's and said in a piteous voice, "They laughed at me, honey. They all laughed at me."

"The jerks," she said, and gave her grandmother a big comforting hug.

"I'm never going back there," said Gran. "I wouldn't be able to face those people."

"It's fine," she said, for lack of anything else to say.

Gran straightened and regained her composure. "So what are you doing out here? Spying on Omar for your newspaper?"

Odelia was taken aback by these words. She thought about denying the charge, but catching Gran's gaze, abandoned this strategy. The old lady might be a little banged up emotionally, but even now she wasn't one to allow the wool to be pulled over her eyes.

"Yeah," she admitted. "That's exactly what I was doing. How did you know?"

"Oh, honey. We've been in the trenches together how many times now? Of course I knew the only reason you joined me last night was to spy out the place and collect material for an article. But why are you sitting here on the outside while you could be an insider?"

"There's this guy I want to talk to. His name is Jason and Max overheard him complaining about Omar and the way he treats him, so I've been hoping to have a word with him. Only I have no idea what he looks like, or even what his last name is."

"Jason Blowhard," said Gran. "He works security for Omar, and it doesn't surprise me that's he's unhappy with the way things are going. He used to be Omar's right-hand man, before being supplanted by Jaqlyn Jones."

"Do you know where he lives? Can you introduce me? I really want to talk to the guy."

Gran hesitated, pulled between loyalty to Omar and affection for her granddaughter.

"You're not going to write some slanderous article about Omar, are you? He's a good dude, even if he doesn't want to marry me."

"I just want to find out everything I can about Soul Science, and write a balanced and objective article," she said, and meant it, too. She didn't have a grudge against Omar, and wasn't planning on doing a hatchet job on the man or his movement.

"Okay," said Gran. "Yeah, I know where he lives. And sure I can introduce you. But if I tell him you're there in your capacity as a reporter your cover will be blown, you do realize that, don't you? And I'll probably get into a heap of trouble with Omar."

"Yeah, I do realize that," said Odelia. "But I've been trying to land an exclusive sit-down with Omar and no dice. So I need to get my information elsewhere."

"If you promise to go easy on Soul Science, I'll get you your exclusive," said Gran. "Omar owes me."

Odelia smiled. "Gran, you're the best."

"Yeah, yeah. Tell that to my future husband who's not to be. Oh, well. It was never going to work between us anyway. I guess he prefers the Scarletts of this world over the likes of little old me, and any man who has the bad taste of falling for Scarlett is a definite no-no. Been there, done that." She smiled at her granddaughter, and it was as if the sun was breaking through the clouds. "Let's you and I go on one of our adventures together, shall we? I need the distraction, and I could use feeling useful again for a change."

"You've got yourself a deal, Gran," said Odelia, and started up the car.

22

$\mathcal{D}$ooley and I were returning from our rendezvous with Kingman when a car stopped next to us and a familiar voice yelled, "Stick 'em up, you punks!"

When I looked up, I found myself staring into the smiling face of Grandma Muffin.

"Just kidding," she said. "Get in, will ya? And make it quick. I haven't got all day."

So Dooley and I got in, and Odelia stomped her foot on the accelerator and soon we were off at a decent clip, on our way to a destination or destinations unknown.

"So what have you guys been up to?" asked Gran, turning to chat.

"We just witnessed the launch of a new movement," I said.

"Yes, Wilbur Vickery and Father Reilly are joining forces to fight Soul Science and get rid of them once and for all," said Dooley, who's never heard of the concept of diplomacy.

Gran frowned. "Francis and Wilbur? Get rid of Soul Science? But why?"

"Father Reilly says Omar is a blasphemer and worships fake gods," I said.

"And Wilbur said that he's a pied piper and he's trying to steal all of Hampton Cove's pets," Dooley added.

"Nonsense," said Gran. "They both must have had a hit on the head to talk such crap. I'll have to have a word with Francis Reilly. Give the old codger a piece of my mind."

"We're actually going to interview one of Omar's key people," said Odelia. "Are you guys game to snoop around while we sit down with him?"

"Oh, sure," I said. I'm always game to snoop around. In fact snooping around is what I do best. It probably constitutes the meaning of my life and is a source of great happiness.

"Why are you dressed like that, Gran?" asked Dooley.

"Like what? Don't you like it?" asked Gran, flicking a speck of dust from her jacket.

"I like it," said Dooley. "But you look like a politician."

"I do, don't I?" said Gran, sounding surprised. "Maybe I should go into politics."

"I think you would make a great politician," said Dooley.

"Please don't encourage her, Dooley," I whispered.

We'd arrived at our destination, and Odelia parked her car in front of the house of our next target.

"Are you sure this is where he lives?" she asked, glancing up at a house that looked a little past its prime. The facade paint was peeling in places, and the windows looked like they needed replacing.

"Yeah, I'm sure. And don't be surprised when a woman my age opens the door. Jason lives with his mom and granny. Three generations under the same roof. Crazy, I know."

She got out, and opened the door so Dooley and I could hop out.

She cracked her knuckles and said, "Let's do this."

She'd been right about an old lady opening the door, and when said old lady caught sight of Gran in her mauve pantsuit, she immediately said, "We don't go in for politics around here," and made to close the door.

Luckily Gran has mastered the technique of gently persuading people to let her in: she placed her foot in the door, then gave it a hearty shove, causing the old lady to yelp in surprise and stagger back.

"Hi there," said Gran. "I don't think we've met before but I'm a proud member of your grandson's church. And in fact I'm here to discuss church matters with him."

The woman's lips tightened, then she yelled, "Jason! Someone from that horrible cult of yours is here to see you!"

A man came stomping down the stairs, and when he saw Gran, his face broke into a wide smile. "Why, Mrs. Muffin. To what do I owe the pleasure?" He was squat, with floppy brown hair, and had the word 'Jason' tattooed on his right cheek.

"You know this lady?" asked his grandmother.

"Yes, I do. She's one of Master Omar's top recruiters."

But his grandmother apparently wasn't as up to date on church matters as her grandson, for she shook her head and said, "Oh, for crying out loud," and shuffled off.

"You have to forgive Gam-Gam," said Jason, blushing a little. "She's getting on in age."

"That's all right," said Gran. "Senile people have rights, too. This is my granddaughter Odelia, by the way. You may remember her from last night's meeting."

"Of course," said Jason, and courteously shook Odelia's hand. "Contrary to Gam-Gam, I never forget a face, especially one as strikingly pretty as yours."

"Cool your jets, buddy,'" said Gran. "Odelia is engaged to a cop."

"Oh," said Jason, and lost some of his spark.

"And these are my cats," said Gran. "The fat red one is

Max and the skinny gray one is Dooley. So can we come in for a chat?"

I was going to formulate a stern rebuke but Gran didn't give me the chance. 'The Fat red one?' Really? Not a very nice thing to say, especially coming from your very own human. But then Gran was in a strange mood. Probably being engaged for a millisecond to a cult leader will do that to a person.

Odelia gestured for us to explore the rest of the house, while she followed Jason into what I assumed was the living room, and Dooley and I did as we were asked and moved along the hallway, following in Jason's irascible Gam-Gam's footsteps.

"What if they don't have pets, Max?" asked Dooley.

"Then we simply get the lay of the land and report back to Odelia on anything we find," I said.

"Gran is acting a little strange, don't you think?"

"Well, I'm glad you noticed," I said. "Did you hear what she just called me?"

"She's not herself, Max. You can't blame people when they're not themselves."

He was probably right, but still. Then again, we were on a mission, and I wasn't going to let my personal feelings impede my responsibilities as a sleuth. So I locked my hurt feelings inside a little box, tucked away the key, and stuck my nose in the air, sniffing around for traces of pets. Unfortunately all I smelled was mold, cabbage, and badly ventilated spaces. This clearly was an old house, and not a very well-maintained one.

Dooley, who'd also been sniffing up a storm, wrinkled his nose. "It smells as if someone died in here," he said finally, and maybe someone had.

We'd arrived at a closed door, and I gave it a gentle push. It yielded to pressure and swung open to reveal the kitchen.

No trace of any pets, though, and I hadn't been able to pick up the scent of one either.

At the kitchen table, Gam-Gam was sitting and slurping from a bowl of soup. A second person was also present, and judging from her age and appearance, I ventured a guess that this was Jason's dear, sweet mother.

She looked up when Dooley and I walked in, and blinked. "How did those get in here?" she asked.

Gam-Gam frowned. "They're that nasty old bird's cats. No idea why she decided to bring them along. The woman is cuckoo if you ask me."

Jason's mom crouched down and tickled me behind my ear. Inadvertently I closed my eyes and started purring. I'm sorry but it's one of those reflex actions that cats have a hard time controlling.

"You're a pudgy ball of fur, aren't you?" she said.

Immediately I stopped purring and opened my eyes to give her as supercilious a look as I could muster on the spur of the moment.

"For your information, I'm not fat and I'm not pudgy," I said. "I'm merely big-boned. Also, before you make the same fatal mistake Gran made, let me set the record straight on another point of contention: I'm not red, I'm blorange. *Blorange*. And yes, it is a color."

"Will you listen to that," said the woman with a smile. "He's a real Chatty Cathy."

"A big yapper, if you ask me," said the older woman, and took another noisy slurp from her soup. "Good thing we talked Jason out of getting cats, Martha," she said. "Otherwise we'd have a couple of those hairballs running around and making a fuss."

"Oh, Mom, you shouldn't say those things about cats. They're noble creatures. Master Omar said so himself."

"Master Omar, Master Omar," grumbled Gam-Gam. "I've

known Omar Carter since he was yea high, so don't you start that Master Omar nonsense with me."

"Shush," said her daughter. "Jason will hear you!"

"And what if he does? He knows how I feel about his precious Omar. If that guy is a god I'm the Queen of Sheba. He's just another fool with delusions of grandeur, and maybe it's time someone told Jason."

"But look how well he's doing. He hasn't touched a drop of alcohol since he joined Soul Science. And I, for one, feel we owe Omar Carter a big debt of gratitude."

"Couldn't he simply have stuck with Alcoholics Anonymous like everybody else?" asked Gam-Gam. "Now we're all tangled up in that damn cult."

"Cult or not, it's done Jason a wealth of good, so let's not rock the boat."

"Easy for you to say. You don't have to sit there night after night and listen to the moron talking a load of twaddle," grumbled the old woman.

Clearly Jason's family had some reservations about their offspring joining Soul Science, and I was straining my ears to hear more when Jason himself came bursting into the kitchen. "Do we have tea? My guests are thirsty."

"Your guests can go to hell," said Gam-Gam.

"Mom!" hissed Martha. "Language!"

"Oh, who cares? I'm old enough to do whatever I damn well please in my own home. And if they want tea they can get it themselves. I'm not going to coddle them."

And with these words, she got up and walked out.

"What's with Gam-Gam?" asked Jason.

"Probably her sciatica acting up again. Better not to pay attention. Now what kind of tea do our guests want?"

23

"*D*o you guys want something to eat?" asked Martha, while her son put the kettle on.

"I wouldn't say no to a piece of sausage," I intimated, perking up. So far this entire trip seemed to have been a bust. No pets to talk to and not much information to glean.

"For me a saucer of milk, if you please," said Dooley politely.

"Poor babies are starving," said Martha, who clearly was a woman with a big heart.

"Mom, don't we have chocolate?" asked Jason. "Vesta is really partial to chocolate."

"Tell that woman she can get her own damn chocolate," said Gam-Gam from the door, staging a surprise return to the scene.

"Gam-Gam!" said Jason with a laugh. "I can't tell my guests to get their own chocolate."

"If you're too chicken to tell them, I will," she said, and made for the door.

Jason uttered a startled yelp and his mother said, "Don't

embarrass Jason in front of his guests, Mom. Just sit down and finish your soup."

The old lady grumbled something under her breath, but still did as she was told.

Jason disappeared again, and in due course I received my piece of sausage and Dooley got his saucer of milk, as ordered. Almost as if Martha could understand us.

Moments later, Jason appeared again. "Do we have pralines? Vesta is partial to pralines."

"To hell with the woman and her pralines!" cried Gam-Gam, getting up, but Martha pushed her back down.

"Look in the fridge. I think we have some left over from your uncle Bernie's birthday."

Jason retrieved the pralines and disappeared again, only to return moments later. "Is that tea ready yet?" he asked, slightly harried. And when his mother handed him the tray with the teapot and cups and saucers, he lifted the lid and sniffed. "What tea is this? Vesta specifically told me she only drinks herbal tea."

"Oh, for crying out loud!" said his grandmother, getting up. "I'll give that fussy old bat a piece of my mind!"

"Sit down, mom," said Martha, and the old lady sat down.

After being assured that only herbal tea was on the menu, Jason disappeared again, only to pop up again five seconds later, like a jack-in-the-box.

"Do we have any oatmeal cookies?"

"Let me get my hands on the woman!" Gam-Gam cried. "I'll give her oatmeal cookies!"

"Be nice, Mom," said Martha, and pushed her mother down onto her seat again. She turned to her son. "No oatmeal cookies, I'm afraid."

"How about a knuckle sandwich?" said Gam-Gam.

"I think I'll pass," said Jason, and popped off again.

"Fun family," said Dooley, having drunk the last drop of milk and licking it from his lips. "And so nice to cats."

"Yeah, very nice," I said, hoping Gam-Gam and Gran would never find themselves in the same room. Probably a minor nuclear explosion would take place.

🐾

"I admire you so much, Vesta," said Jason, unabashedly gushing over Odelia's grandmother. "The way you single-handedly managed to bring in all of those followers. And the way you convinced your family to join the church. I wish I could do the same."

"Your family isn't keen on joining your church?" asked Odelia.

They'd taken a seat in the living room. A couple of chairs had been placed around a small table, and in a corner a couch and two armchairs were positioned in front of an old television, all of them festooned with doilies. On the walls framed pictures of Jason's family were in evidence, knickknacks liberally strewn across every available surface.

"No, my family isn't as interested in the spirit as I am," said Jason sadly. "They regularly attend Soul Science meetings, but I think they only do it to humor me."

"I heard your grandmother refer to Soul Science as a cult?" asked Gran.

"Yeah, Gam-Gam is not exactly Master Omar's biggest champion."

"She looks like a real pistol."

"She's something else," Jason agreed, inadvertently darting a glance at the door, as if dreading the prospect of his grandmother joining them. "So what brings you here?" he asked, then: "Oh, where are my manners? Do you want something to drink?"

"Tea, maybe," said Gran.

"Nothing for me," said Odelia, who didn't want to inconvenience Jason or his family.

"What kind of tea do you prefer?" asked Jason, getting up.

"Anything you've got," said Gran. "But if you have herbal tea, that would be great."

"Be right back," he said with a smile, and was off like a rabbit, only to return moments later with an apologetic expression on his face. "Tea will be a few moments."

"That's fine," said Odelia. "The reason we're here is because I'm actually a reporter, and I'm writing an article on Soul Science."

"Only this is going to be a very positive article," said Vesta, casting a pointed look at her granddaughter. "Isn't that right, Odelia?"

"Yes, a very positive article," she dutifully confirmed.

"You're a reporter?" asked Jason, suddenly nervous. "I-I didn't know that."

"She's a very honest and conscientious reporter," Gran clarified. "Not one of them overly critical ones who like to twist your words and invent a lot of stuff you never said."

"Yeah, I don't go in for that sort of thing," said Odelia.

"Okay," said Jason, now wringing his hands. "So... what is it you want to know?"

"Well, Soul Science is pretty new," said Odelia. "And people are wondering where it suddenly came from, and what Master Omar's intentions are. In general I think people simply want to understand."

"Okay. Um..."

"Maybe you can start by telling us how you got involved with Soul Science?"

"Oh, well, um..." He glanced from Odelia to Vesta, and swallowed convulsively. "So, um... Are you going to print everything I tell you? Is that how this works?"

"Look, if you want, we can conduct this entire interview off the record," said Odelia, who sensed sales resistance. "In which case I'll simply use whatever you tell me as background information, and your name will never be mentioned, nor will the fact that you talked to me today."

This seemed to please the young man, for he visibly relaxed. "I would like that. Not that I have something to hide or anything. It's just that..." He glanced at the door, and said, "Please excuse me for a moment." And was gone again.

"Nervous type, isn't he?" said Gran. "He moves so fast he's like a blur."

"There's a story here, Gran," said Odelia. "I can feel it."

"Do you think they've got chocolate? I would kill for a piece of chocolate right now. I skipped dinner, thinking Omar was going to splurge on me, and now I'm starving."

"Wait until we're home," Odelia suggested. "We're guests. We can't ask for food."

"Yeah, you're probably right." Jason walked in and she said, "You don't happen to have any chocolate, do you? I'm diabetic and if I don't get my sugar levels up I might die."

Odelia rolled her eyes. Looked like Gran was herself again.

Finally plied with tea and refreshments, the interview could proceed.

"I'll tell you the truth, but only if you promise not to print anything about this in your newspaper," said Jason.

"I promise," said Odelia.

"And I'm keeping you to that," said Gran, munching on a delicious-looking praline.

"I'm an addict," said Jason with a deep sigh. "Alcohol. I joined Alcoholics Anonymous at Father Reilly's and one of the people present introduced me to Soul Science."

"Recruited straight from Father Reilly's flock, huh?" said

Gran, grinning. "I'll bet he didn't like that. Joining the competition."

"It wasn't like that. Father Reilly doesn't even know about any of this. I just... I needed something more than the twelve-step program and Soul Science offered me just that. It gave me a group of like-minded people that I can now call my friends. Master Omar knows all about my past, and he supports me one hundred percent."

"What do think about Jaqlyn Jones?" asked Odelia, and watched Jason's face cloud over.

"Um... he's one of our most prominent members. Hard-working. Great recruiter."

"Do you also consider him your friend?" asked Odelia, probing gently.

"No. Well, yes..." He coughed. "Honestly? Jaqlyn is not my favorite person in the world. I used to sit at Master Omar's table before Jaqlyn joined the church. In fact I used to be Omar's principal apostle, so to speak. Only Jaqlyn took over that role and pretty much pushed me out."

"Must have been tough on you," said Odelia.

"It still is. I've been relegated to a role in the background, and I'm still adjusting."

"Jaqlyn Jones is scum," said Gran, picking another praline from the tray.

"I wouldn't go so far as that," said Jason. "But he has a manipulative streak. He knows just what to say and how and when to say it, and he likes to bask in the limelight."

"These pralines are great," said Gran, smacking her lips. "Got any more?"

Immediately Jason jumped up. "One sec," he said, and was gone again.

"Gran! You can't eat these people's food! It's not okay!"

"Why not? It's great food. Besides, I need it for my diabetes."

"You don't have diabetes!"

"I don't? Are you sure?"

Suddenly the door flew open and Jason's grandmother appeared. She didn't look happy. "Who do you think you are, coming in here and eating my favorite pralines?!"

"They're good," Gran confirmed. "You've got great taste, old biddy."

She hadn't struck the right note. The old lady shook her fist. "You cultists are all the same. A bunch of smarmy blood-suckers. Well I'm here to tell you that the Blowhard restaurant is closed for business! Get out, you freeloading old bat! Out!"

"Mom!" Jason's mother cried. "You can't treat our guests like that!"

"They're not guests, they're cultists! Get lost, ye Satan's spawn—out of my house!"

"Who are you calling Satan's spawn, you crazy old cow?" said Gran, now also on her feet and going toe to toe with the other woman.

"You're the crazy old cow, you crazy old hag!"

"Who are you calling a crazy old hag, you crazy old crone?!"

"You're the crazy old crone, you crazy old pest!"

"Who are you calling a crazy old pest, you—"

Odelia had the feeling this could go on for a little while, so she took her grandmother's arm, and said, "Come on, Gran. We're leaving."

"You ate all my pralines!" Gam-Gam cried, noticing the little pile of shiny empty wrappers. "Those were my pralines!"

"I'm diabetic, what's your excuse!" said Gran.

"Come on," said Odelia, and forcibly took her grand-mother's arm and steered her toward the corridor. "Thank you for your hospitality, Jason. I'm sorry about the pralines."

They were already out on the street, on their way to the car, when Odelia suddenly remembered that her cats were still inside. But she needn't have worried: as she turned back, the front door opened and Max and Dooley came scampering out the front door, as if ejected by force. They both seemed well-pleased and brimming with Jason's food.

Odelia shook her head. How extremely embarrassing.

And she hadn't even learned anything new.

he day had finally arrived: Jaqlyn and Francine Jones's garden party was upon us and the turnout was impressive. Of course Odelia was there, in her capacity both as a Hampton Covian but also as a reporter fulfilling her promise to cover both Jaqlyn Jones and Soul Science in a series of future articles. But the rest of the Poole clan had also decided to put in an appearance, which from Tex's side was with some reluctance.

Even though Tex had accepted Jaqlyn's offered olive branch, he probably would never be the other doctor's biggest or most vocal fan.

The only one who'd decided to sit this one out was Gran, who was still recovering from the humiliation at Soul Science and didn't feel like facing the same people so soon.

Dooley and I had accepted Odelia's suggestion to sniff around and see what we could discover. I didn't expect much, except maybe a few tasty morsels falling from a tray of one of the waiters hired by the Joneses to officiate the social event of the season.

This was Jaqlyn and Francine's official introduction to

the Hampton Cove social scene, a little belatedly, as half of Hampton Cove had already passed through his office by now, and so the backyard of Casa Jones was buzzing with activity. There was a clown, magician and bouncy castle for the kids, and plenty of food and drinks for the grownups.

For the pets, unfortunately, no provisions had been made, but I tried not to let that get me down.

"Do you think Master Omar will show up, and Master Sharif?" asked Dooley.

We were strategically positioned near the food table, inveterate optimists that we both are, and eyeing the humans closely. My money was on an elderly lady who seemed to have trouble guiding hors d'oeuvres into her mouth, and kept dropping them. The moment her husband gave up picking them up I was ready to pounce on those remnants.

"I don't think so," I said, never taking my eyes off the lady. "He'd face too much scrutiny coming to an event like this."

"I bet he'll show up," said Dooley. "He's still building his church, and needs all the followers he can get."

"He has all the followers he can get," I argued. "Didn't you see the size of that meeting? The place was packed to capacity. Not an empty seat in the house."

"He can always use more," said Dooley, not unreasonably.

He was right, of course. No self-respecting leader of a church will thumb his nose at a few more followers, especially when he's an up-and-coming guru like Omar Carter.

Brutus and Harriet now joined us, and I could detect several more cats roaming the grounds, clearly eager to get in on some of the action, too.

"So how was the meeting last night?" I asked.

Harriet looked as if she hadn't slept much, so it was safe to assume she'd joined Sharif's most recent meeting. Dooley and I had decided to skip this one, as we'd both had just about all the soul science we could stomach. Plus, with resistance building throughout the local cat community, as evidenced by Kingman's opposition, we'd decided we were going to be Switzerland and remain strictly neutral. Though Dooley did mention he thought Master Sharif was a wonderful and most skillful sleep inducer.

Odelia, likewise, had decided not to attend her second meeting in two nights, being supportive of her grandmother, who was now completely over her newfound religion. And even Marge had said the previous meeting hadn't given her what she'd expected and she wasn't going back for a refill.

"It was... nice," said Harriet, which surprised me, because before she'd only ever spoken about Sharif in superlatives.

"Nice?" I said. "Not earth-shattering or life-changing or revolutionary?"

"Oh, don't you start, Max," she said, a little grumpily. "Where's the food? I didn't have breakfast." And off she went, in search of something edible.

Dooley and I both turned to Brutus, looking for an explanation of Harriet's sudden lack of religious fervor and spiritual prowess.

He gave us a wide grin in return. "I think she's over Soul Science, you guys," he said, not trying to hide his elation. "Last night she had another run-in with Shanille, and this time Sharif took Shanille's side. I think Harriet is ready to tear up her Soul Science membership card."

"What did they argue about?" I asked, like any good sleuth digging for the telling clue.

"Shanille said that we should all focus our attention solely on developing our spiritual sides from now on—taking care of our souls and completely ignoring our attachments to the material world. Which means weekly fasts, no more daily grooming, and most definitely no pet salons, manicures, pedicures, hair styling or even... nookie."

"Nookie?" asked Dooley, confused. "Is that like a cookie?"

"Yes, Dooley," I said. "A nookie is a kind of cookie."

"Oh," he said, nodding. "But why? Doesn't Shanille like cookies?"

Brutus shrugged. "Shanille is determined to go to extremes to show Master Sharif that she's completely on board with Soul Science's mission to make all cats everywhere more spiritual. She's trying to outfollow even its most fanatic followers."

"And Harriet didn't agree?" I asked.

"Harriet didn't agree," he agreed. "She felt that Shanille was specifically targeting her with that crack about no more pet salons and no more nookie. She knows how much Harriet likes her regular visits to the salon and her, um..." He darted a quick glance at Dooley. "And her... nookies."

"So that's it for Soul Science," I said. "Gran is out, and now Harriet is out, too. I'll bet it won't be long before the rest of cat choir follows suit, and only Shanille will be left."

"Which means we need a new conductor for cat choir," said Brutus. "And guess who's decided to put in his candidacy?"

It was a tough question to answer. "Um... Missy?" I said.

"No."

"Misty?"

"No!"

"Tigger?"

"Max, it's me!" said Brutus. "I'm going to be cat choir's new conductor. With Shanille gone, someone needs to step up and take responsibility, and I've decided that I'm the right cat for the job."

"But you don't know the first thing about conducting," I pointed out.

"How hard can it be! You just wave your paw and the choir does the rest. I talked it over with Harriet last night, and she agreed wholeheartedly. 'Go for it, Brutus,' were her exact words. 'You can do it, sugar plum.'"

"Don't tell me. She made you promise to let her sing a solo every single night."

"Well, duh. She is cat choir's most gifted singer."

I wouldn't go as far as that. In fact there wasn't a single cat in cat choir who could actually sing. I don't know if you've ever heard cats caterwauling in the middle of the night, but they rarely follow a pre-conceived script or musical score. Andrew Lloyd Webber himself could write a catchy tune and personally hand them the pages of sheet music and they'd simply toss it in the trash and go off script. I wasn't going to spoil Brutus's big moment, though, for he looked happier than I'd seen him in days.

"I don't expect every member of cat choir to be there tonight," said Brutus, showing he'd given the matter a measure of thought, "but eventually they'll all come back."

"And what if Shanille returns and demands her old job back?" I asked.

"Then we'll put the matter to a vote. Cat choir is a democracy, not a dictatorship."

I thought Brutus was courting trouble with his bold move, but as I said, he looked so happy I didn't want to rain on his parade.

So instead I clapped him on the back and said, "Well, congratulations, my friend. I will watch your future career with great interest."

And I probably would have said a lot more on the subject if not Francine Jones had suddenly burst onto the scene and bellowed, "Has anyone seen my husband? Has anyone seen Jaqlyn? He's gone!"

---

*O*delia had been looking for Jaqlyn everywhere. She wanted a word with the man. But thus far he'd proved a tough guy to pin down. She'd caught glimpses of him throughout the afternoon, smiling and joking with some of his guests, then carrying a tray of champagne glasses, then assisting his wife in placing extra chairs for some of the elderly.

But each time she'd made a beeline for him, he'd vanished again in the proverbial puff of smoke.

"The guy is like a ghost," she complained after she'd missed him a third time.

"You'll catch him eventually," said Chase, who had complete faith in her abilities as a pinner-downer of tough-to-pin-down doctors.

"Maybe you can give it a shot," she said now. "You're much better at catching people than I am."

"When I see him I'll collar him for you," he promised. "The only question is: handcuffs or no handcuffs? What do you reckon?"

She slapped him lightly on the arm. "Wise guy. You know

how important it is for me to talk to Jaqlyn."

"Important for your newspaper, or for your dad?" he asked, cocking an eyebrow.

"Both," she said. "I want him to tell me exactly why he's been poaching my dad's patients. Does he really intend to put him out of business, or have people suddenly and mysteriously gone off my dad for some reason?"

Uncle Alec had joined them, having snatched two glasses of champagne from a passing waiter's tray. "Great stuff," he said as he took a sip. "Whatever his faults, Jaqlyn doesn't skimp on the goodies."

"If he took over half my dad's patients he can afford it," said Odelia, glancing around for a sign of the elusive doctor.

"I received another complaint about the guy," said Uncle Alec. "Lately it seems to rain complaints."

"Another neighbor whose tires he slashed?" asked Chase.

"No, this time it's a patient's dad. Claims Jaqlyn misdiagnosed his daughter and only through some miracle did she escape with her life."

That got Odelia's attention. "Are you serious?"

Uncle Alec nodded. "Apparently this young lady suffered from a severe headache, but when she told Jaqlyn he simply gave her paracetamol and said she'd be fine in a day or two. Only the headache got worse and so they finally took her to the IC. Turns out she had a brain tumor. They immediately operated on her and she'll recover. It was touch and go, though. A couple more days and she wouldn't have made it."

"But that's terrible!" said Odelia.

"Yeah, her dad wasn't too happy about it. Said he's considering a medical malpractice suit."

Suddenly Francine Jones came walking out of the house, looking a little harried. "Has anyone seen my husband?" she yelled over the din. "Has anyone seen Jaqlyn?"

Conversations halted, and all eyes turned to her.

"What's wrong?" asked Mayor Charlene Butterwick, who was closest to the woman.

"I can't seem to find him anywhere," said Francine, helplessly lifting her hands.

"I'm sure he's around here somewhere," said Mayor Butterwick, and raised her voice. "Has anyone seen our host?"

People were laughing, thinking it was some kind of joke, but judging from the expression on Francine's face it clearly wasn't.

"Looks like you're not the only one who can't pin the man down," said Chase.

Odelia's mom and dad, who'd been chatting with Ted and Marcie Trapper, their neighbors, came drifting over. "What's going on?" asked Mom.

"Our hostess has lost our host," Uncle Alec put the situation in a nutshell.

A statuesque beauty, dressed in a stunning red dress, came walking out of the house and Francine immediately accosted her. "You!" she said. "Where is my husband?"

"How should I know," said the woman, visibly taken aback.

"I know all about you!" said Francine. "I've known for weeks! Is he upstairs? Did you just have sex with my husband in my own bedroom?"

"You're crazy, lady," said the woman.

"Who's that?" asked Chase.

"Monica Chanting," said Odelia. "Wife of Garvin Chanting, landscaper."

"You did, didn't you!" Francine screamed, and launched herself at Monica, nails out. Monica uttered a loud scream, and knocked Francine back, landing the latter on her tush. Like a coiled spring, Francine got up again, and went on the attack, eager to draw blood.

Uncle Alec quickly handed his champagne glasses to Odelia, and hurried forward, bodily inserting himself between the two women. Chase then took hold of Francine while Uncle Alec inspected Monica's face, which was sporting a slash across the cheek.

"It's just a scratch," Monica said. "But the woman is crazy. She should be arrested."

"Can you take a look at this, Tex?" asked Uncle Alec. "She's bleeding something bad."

"Can you get my medical bag from the car, honey?" asked Dad, and handed his car keys to Odelia.

Hurrying away, Odelia moved along the swath of lawn separating Jaqlyn's house from his neighbor Barney Sowman's, and out onto the street, where Dad's car was parked right behind Odelia's. She checked the backseat, but when she didn't see the medical bag in question, decided to look in the trunk. The moment she opened it, she reeled back.

There, staring up at her with lifeless eyes, was Jaqlyn.

And he looked very dead indeed.

Her first reflex was to close the trunk again, but just then Officer Sarah Flunk and her boyfriend arrived, and when she saw the dead body, Sarah immediately said, "Better step away from the car, Odelia. Don't touch anything. Where is your uncle?"

Mutedly, Odelia gestured to the party, where a DJ had just launched Taylor Swift's *Look What You Made Me Do*.

"Go and get Chief Alec for me," Sarah told her boyfriend, who hurried away. "Is this your car?" she asked Odelia, a distinct edge to her voice, her hand inadvertently moving to her belt, as if reaching for her gun.

"No, it's... my dad's," she heard herself say, and Sarah drew in a gasp of shock.

---

26

*W*hen people start screaming, you know that either their host has just told them he unexpectedly ran out of booze, or has managed to get himself killed. In this case the latter explanation, however unlikely, appeared to be the correct one.

Odelia, when she returned from her errand of mercy, looked pale as a sheet, and when she spoke the next words, they took us all by surprise.

"Jaqlyn... is dead," she said, then cut a sad look to her father, who was still waiting for the necessary medical supplies to attend to the scratch on Monica Chanting's face, and added, "I just found his body in the trunk of your car, Dad."

Great was everyone's consternation at these words, and a psychologist, had one been present, would have had a field day tabulating the different responses from those present.

Tex stared at his daughter stupidly, and asked, "Why the trunk of my car?" as if in his expert opinion this was the last place one should ever put a dead body.

Marge said, "Tex? Did you do this?"

To which Tex immediately responded with a pointed, "Do what?"

Uncle Alec, meanwhile, who'd been restraining Francine, found that his job description had changed from restrainer to nurse, as Francine promptly collapsed.

Chase, meanwhile, had the presence of mind to place a heavy hand on his future father-in-law's shoulder and declare, "I'm sorry to have to tell you this, Tex, but I guess you're under arrest."

Nothing personal, his expression seemed to suggest. Just one of those things. And who could blame him? If dead bodies are found in trunks of cars, it's usually those in ownership of those cars that have put them there.

"What's going on, Max?" asked Dooley, who had a hard time following the quickly evolving events.

"Jaqlyn Jones is dead and his body was just found in Tex's car," I said, bringing him up to speed on the latest. "And Chase is now in the process of arresting Tex for murder."

"But... he can't do that," said Dooley, looking aghast. "Tex is family."

"Chase is a cop," I reminded him. "And cops are legally obliged to arrest killers, even if they are members of their family. That's what they teach them at the police academy."

"But... can't he turn a blind eye just this once?"

I glanced around at the dozens of onlookers, all gleefully rubbernecking.

"Not if all of Hampton Cove is watching your every move," I said, "including the mayor."

Mayor Butterwick, who'd looked as shocked as her loyal subjects, now seemed to come out of her temporary paralysis and started barking orders. "Odelia, call an ambulance. Alec, cordon off the crime scene. Chase, take Tex into custody." Then she glanced around and yelled, "No one move! You're all staying put!"

This was all people needed to start dispersing. It's a thing called group dynamics. But they hadn't counted on Charlene Butterwick, who yelled, "Anyone move, I'll have you arrested for obstruction of justice. And don't think I won't do it. I've seen your faces!"

And she did. Any politician worth their salt is familiar with the names and faces of their constituents, and Charlene definitely was worth her salt, and her pepper, too.

"I don't like this, Max," said Dooley now. "I don't want Tex to go to prison."

"I don't like it either, Dooley," I intimated. "But if Tex really did kill Jaqlyn, he probably should go to prison."

"But Jaqlyn wasn't a nice person."

"You mean he deserved to be killed?"

"Well…" Dooley wavered. "I guess not," he finally conceded. "Or maybe just a little."

"You can't kill a person just a little, Dooley. Either you kill them or you don't."

"I guess so," he said, sounding sad.

We watched on as Chase led a stupefied Tex away, Uncle Alec removed himself from the scene, speaking orders into his phone, and Odelia gave instructions to the ambulance people, presumably to revive Francine and take care of Monica. There probably wasn't a whole lot they could do for Jaqlyn.

Brutus and Harriet came hurrying up, Brutus with a piece of chicken filet dangling from his lips and Harriet with lips smeared with red currant sauce for some reason. They'd clearly taken up position near the food table and had done themselves well.

"What's going on?" asked Harriet.

I was ready to repeat my earlier report but Dooley beat me to it. "Tex wanted to kill Jaqlyn just a little bit but overdid it and now Jaqlyn is dead and Tex will go to prison."

"What?!!!" Brutus cried, and to indicate how shook up he was by this bulletin from the front lines, dropped the piece of chicken and didn't even bother to pick it up again.

"Tex? Killed Jaqlyn?" asked Harriet, also looking extremely distraught.

"Sadly, yes," I confirmed. "Chase just arrested him, though not wholeheartedly," I quickly added, to make it clear the cop wasn't one of your devil-may-care arresters.

Odelia crouched down and absentmindedly stroked my fur, something she tends to do when times are tough and she's not feeling on top of the world. It seems to relax her.

"Bad business," I said commiseratively.

"The worst," she agreed, then got up to comfort her mother, who was looking shell-shocked, and probably in need of medical assistance herself.

"I say Jaqlyn had it coming," said Brutus now, another one whose moral compass was a little out of whack.

"You can't say that, Brutus," I said. "No one deserves to die. Not even doctors who steal unto half your patients and say nasty things behind your back."

"Did Jaqlyn say nasty things behind Tex's back?" asked Brutus.

"That's what I heard."

Kingman had come waddling up. He looked appropriately grave. "Tough day," he announced. "The day when the law starts arresting good people like Tex is the day..." He thought for a moment, then finished with, "... well, not a good day, that's for sure."

"Did you know that Jaqlyn had been talking smack behind Tex's back?" asked Brutus.

"Oh, sure. Misty told me two nights ago how she overheard Jaqlyn tell her human that Tex was past his prime and making so many mistakes it was a miracle he hadn't killed a patient yet. And Buster said his human had stopped going to

Tex after meeting Jaqlyn on the street and being told that Tex never even finished medical school. Can you imagine? Jaqlyn said Tex was entirely self-taught and had learned the trade by dissecting rats."

"But... why didn't you tell us?!" Harriet cried. "You should have told us, Kingman!"

The cat looked at us dumbly. "But... I thought you knew. I thought everybody knew."

Oh, boy. If this was true, and Tex knew, he had a big fat motive for murder.

27

*V*esta, who'd decided to stay home from the Jones garden party, heard the news the way most people in Hampton Cove heard it: through the grapevine. In her case she'd been removing greenfly from her precious roses when suddenly she became aware of the sound of heavy breathing. When she looked up, she saw that the breather was none other than Marcie Trapper, and judging from the woman's sparkling eyes, flushed face and flaring nostrils, she was about to spill some particularly startling piece of news.

Without awaiting permission, Marcie burst out, "Tex has been arrested for murder!"

Vesta narrowed her eyes at her neighbor, then sniffed the air, trying to determine if Marcie had been hitting the bottle a little too hard. She knew Marcie and Ted had planned to go to the Jones bash, and knowing her neighbors also knew that their capacity for imbibing alcoholic beverages was above the norm.

"Have you been drinking?" she asked therefore.

"Yes, but who cares? Didn't you hear what I just said? Tex

has been arrested for the murder of Jaqlyn Jones! Odelia herself found him in the trunk of her dad's car. Dead! Apparently he'd been hit over the head and the body was still warm when she found him!"

"Huh," said Vesta. This was news. "They arrested Tex?"

"Chase did. Carted him off to the station house *tout de suite*, as the French say. Can you imagine what Marge must be feeling right now? She looked devastated. I tried to talk to her but she only spoke in monosyllables. Poor Marge. I've never seen her like that."

"Right," said Vesta, removing her gardening gloves, her gardening apron and her gardening scarf. Then, without another word, she made for the great indoors.

"Where are you going?" Marcie yelled, clearly disappointed with her neighbor's tepid response.

"To clear my son-in-law's name!" Vesta yelled back. "He didn't do it, Marcie."

"Are you sure?"

"As sure as I am that you're blotto!"

&

Odelia, under normal circumstances so rational and sane, was shaken up. She was used to investigating all manner of crime, but suddenly felt unequal to the task of investigating this particular crime. Her dad? A murderer? It was hard to fathom.

"I should have seen it coming," said her mother. "He told me just the other night that something had to be done. But how could I have known he planned to kill Jaqlyn!"

"He's been under a lot of pressure lately," Odelia agreed. "But did he think he could get away with this? I mean, he asked me to get his bag from the car. Did he think I wouldn't see the body?"

"He hasn't been thinking straight. He must have killed Jaqlyn in a moment of insanity, stuck him in his car and forgotten all about it." Marge directed an anxious look at her daughter. "I hope the judge will be lenient when he sets your dad's sentence. I hope he'll understand that under normal circumstances Tex would never do something like this."

"We have to get him a good lawyer."

"The best."

"I'll chip in if you can't afford one, Mom," said Odelia. "We'll all chip in."

"Financially it's been a tough couple of months," Mom agreed, "but I can always sell the house, or take a second mortgage."

"We'll get through this," Odelia promised her mother.

The ambulance had arrived twenty minutes earlier and taken care of Francine and Monica. More police officers had been dispatched, and had undertaken the task of taking witness statements from all of those present, which was an undertaking that was still ongoing, as half of Hampton Cove had shown up for Jaqlyn's and Francine's party.

And as Odelia and Marge sat commiserating, suddenly Gran walked up, a resolute look on her face. "Well?" she said, taking a wide-legged stance in front of her daughter and granddaughter. "Why aren't you talking to people? Finding out what happened?"

"We know what happened," said Odelia. "Dad snapped and hit Jaqlyn over the head with something and stuffed him in the trunk of his car."

"Bullcrap!" said Vesta. "Tex didn't do diddly squat. That man is incapable of murder. No, someone else killed that no-good piece of human trash and is trying to frame Tex."

"As much as I appreciate your faith in my husband," said Mom, "I don't think—"

"Exactly! You're not thinking straight, and I don't blame

you. If my husband got caught with a dead body in his car I'd jump to conclusions as well. Although, in Jack's case I might have turned him in myself, but that's not important right now. What's important is that we need to move fast. Marcie told me the body was still warm, so the murder must have happened just before you found the dead shmuck, correct?"

"I guess so," said Odelia, dragging her mind back to the moment she'd discovered Jaqlyn's body. The memory wasn't a pleasant one, as she kept seeing the man's dead eyes staring up at her.

"Which means the killer is still here," said Gran, glancing around. "So let's get cracking."

"What do you mean?" asked Odelia, confused.

"This is not our first rodeo, hun. You and I have caught killers before. Well, let's catch this one while he still thinks he's gotten away with it. Let's move quick!"

Odelia got up from the garden bench she and her mother had sunk onto after the devastating news had unfolded before their very eyes. "Are you sure?" she asked now, a tiny flicker of hope suddenly surging in her bosom.

"Of course I'm sure! Tex and I may not always see eye to eye, but that doesn't mean I'm not fond of the poor fish. And I'll be damned if I'm going to let him rot in prison for a crime he didn't commit. Come on, missy. We've got a killer to catch and a reputation to save."

And with these words, she was off in the direction of the Jones residence.

*W*e'd all overheard Gran talk to her granddaughter like a Dutch uncle, and her words had inspired me.

"Gran is right," I said. "Tex would never do such a thing. The man is inherently good and incapable of an act of pure evil."

"Maybe he didn't mean to kill Jaqlyn," Harriet suggested. "Maybe it was an accident."

"I think I know what happened," said Brutus. "Tex is just like me: he doesn't know his own strength. He probably just wanted to teach the guy a lesson and gave him a light tap on the head. Only he overdid it and found himself with a dead body on his hands."

"So he panicked and stuffed him in the trunk of his car," Harriet finished the story.

"Doubtful," said Kingman. "Tex doesn't exactly look like the strongman type to me."

"He's a doctor, and doctors are surprisingly muscular," said Brutus, reluctant to abandon his neat little theory without a fight.

"Brutus is right," said Harriet, coming to her mate's support. "Doctors need to be able to lift patients with a finger so they can twirl them around and change their bedding and such. Or lift them up when they've managed to land themselves on the bedroom floor."

"You're thinking of nurses," I said. "That's exactly the kind of strenuous activity nurses engage in."

"No, I'm thinking of doctors," Harriet insisted. "Just look at Vena," she added as a possibly decisive argument. "She's as strong as an ox. Maybe even two or three oxen."

"Vena is a vet," I pointed out. "And vets need to be able to pull a calf from a cow, which is why they're so strong. I've never seen Tex pull a calf from a cow."

"Maybe he pulls calves from cows when no one is watching?" Dooley suggested.

"I still think he did it," said Brutus. "Why else would the body be in his car?"

It was one of those aspects which are a little hard to move past, and any jury of Tex's peers would probably think along the same lines.

"Look, it doesn't matter what we think," I argued. "If Gran says he didn't do it, at the very least we should join the investigation and try to clear the man's name. We owe him that much, wouldn't you agree?"

"We could always talk to witnesses," Harriet allowed. "Ask around and gather the facts."

"I'll help you guys," said Kingman. "I don't have much else to do right now, and I kinda like Tex. He once removed a splinter from my paw and I feel like I owe him for that."

"Let's split up," I suggested. "Dooley and I will look for witnesses out on the street, while you guys talk to pets who were at the party."

"Deal," said Kingman, who looked excited to be joining us

on his first-ever investigation. And as Brutus and Harriet pottered off in the direction of the garden, Kingman asked, "So how do I do this, Max? Do I look for specific clues? Fingerprints and footprints and cigar stubs and all that sort of thing? Or do I ask a bunch of seemingly innocuous questions, then walk away only to turn back and say, 'Just one more thing?'"

"No, you just talk to any pet you find, and ask them if they saw something that might shed some light on what happened here this afternoon. We're trying to build a timeline of events. To know who was where, when, with who, and did what to whom, how and why."

He nodded along as I spoke. "Uh-huh. Uh-huh. Could you repeat that one more time?"

"You ask who did what to whom when, where, how and why," Dooley explained.

"Oh-kay," said Kingman, his eyes glazing over somewhat. "Gotcha. So I figure out who was where when they did what to whom… why?"

"No, you try to figure out who was where when whatever happened to whoever for whatever reason," said Dooley helpfully.

Kingman looked mystified. "Wow. This sleuthing stuff is a lot harder than it looks on TV. You know what? I'll just ask folks what they think happened. I'm pretty sure they'll tell me something useful."

"Or you can do that," I agreed.

Dooley and I walked back to the street, and saw that Uncle Alec was instructing his officers to festoon the scene with that nice yellow police tape that adds that cheerful touch to crime scenes, while an ambulance stood nearby, and also Abe Cornwall's car.

Abe is our county coroner, and whenever a dead body is

found he can't seem to stay away. He was all over Tex's car now, along with a couple of people dressed in white from top to toe for some reason, who were dusting the car and taking plenty of pictures.

A man had come walking up, and now addressed Uncle Alec. He was a large man with a protruding belly and a surprisingly zippy demeanor, given the circumstances.

"So it's true, huh? Jaqlyn Jones finally met his maker."

"Barney," said Uncle Alec. "I was just on my way over to see you. Did you by any chance see what happened?"

"There was a big to-do," said Barney, fondling a yellow handlebar mustache of which he seemed particularly proud. "But of course I wasn't invited, which was to be expected."

"No, I mean did you happen to see Tex and Jaqlyn going at it?"

"Tex? You mean your brother-in-law? He did this?"

"Yeah, he did. Slugged the man and stuffed his body in the trunk of his car."

Barney took off his New York Rangers ball cap and scratched his scalp. "Way to go, Doctor Poole. I've always liked Tex. I have to tell you I didn't think he had it in him."

"But you didn't see the fight?"

"No, sir, I sure didn't. If I had I would have intervened. Lord knows I hated Jaqlyn's guts, but beating him to death seems a little harsh. I would have simply taken him to court if I were in Doc Poole's shoes."

"So you heard about the animosity that existed between the two doctors?"

"Who hadn't? It was a well-known fact Jaqlyn was doing a real number on the Doc. Tarnishing his reputation and stealing his patients. But like I said, that's no reason to go and beat him over the head with... What did he use, exactly, if I may ask?" There was a touch of wistfulness in his voice, as if secretly regretting he hadn't thought of the same thing.

"We haven't found the murder weapon yet," said Uncle Alec. "But we'll find it," he was quick to assure the other man.

"I'd go for aluminum," said Barney, offering an expert's opinion. "Aluminum baseball bat. One nice whack and it's game over. I wouldn't use wood. Wood cracks. You don't want that."

"Okay," said Alec, eyeing the man a little strangely.

"Or a billy club. A metal one. Limit the point of impact."

This time Alec didn't respond, but merely stared at the other man.

"Of course there's a lot to be said for your plain old hammer," Barney allowed magnanimously. "You can call me old-fashioned but a good hammer is like a best friend. Always there when you need it. Never fails to get the job done, if you see what I mean."

"I think Barney is sad that Tex killed Jaqlyn first," Dooley commented, and I thought he was probably right.

We searched around for any pet witnesses, and found a small dog of the Schnauzer variety following the buzz of activity on his street with marked interest.

So we sidled up to the hirsute canine, careful not to startle him or her, and introduced ourselves.

"Hi, my name is Max," I said, "and this is my friend Dooley. We're Odelia Poole's cats. Odelia is investigating the murder of Jaqlyn Jones and has asked us to participate in the investigation."

"Oh, hi," said the Schnauzer. "I'm Jack, and that's my human over there." He gestured with his snout to Barney, who now stood pontificating about different types of hammers and their respective advantages and disadvantages in dispensing with annoying neighbors.

"So did you know Jaqlyn?" I asked, opening my inquiries with a softball question.

"I knew of him," said Jack. "Barney didn't like him very

much, and frankly neither did I. You see, Barney possesses a nice little plot of land located right behind Jaqlyn's house, only Jaqlyn forbade him access, and they've been fighting about it for a while now. Only a couple of days ago Jaqlyn put a spiky thing on the track and destroyed Barney's tires. Barney wasn't happy. In fact he told me he was going to kill Jaqlyn first chance he got."

This startled me to some degree. "He actually said that?"

"Oh, yes," said Jack. "He said a lot more, too, but most of that were swear words, and I don't like to repeat them to two nice and polite cats such as yourselves."

"That's very kind of you, Jack," said Dooley appreciatively.

"Don't mention it. One does what one can to spread a little sweetness and light in the world, and repeating bad words isn't part of that endeavor."

"So... do you think Barney went ahead and did as he promised?" I asked, crossing my fingers and hoping Jack wouldn't suddenly go all reticent on us. Some pets are like that, especially dogs. They'll defend their humans regardless of the laws of man.

"I doubt it," said Jack. "Barney is all talk and little action. Most people who curse a lot are. They release tension by cursing, whereas people who never say a bad word but bottle it all up inside? They're the ones you have to watch out for. They're the ones who suddenly explode and slay six in a homicidal frenzy."

I gulped a little, and so did Dooley. "You seem to know a lot about the subject," I said.

"Barney and I watch a lot of crime shows," the dog said with a smile that lifted his hairy beard and mustache. "Seated side by side on the big couch we watch crime shows every night."

"You like your human a lot, don't you?" I said.

"Oh, sure, I love the guy. Barney is a little rough around the edges maybe, but he's got a heart of gold. Dogs can sense it when humans have their hearts in the right place. But then I guess cats can, too." He gave me an earnest look. "You probably knew the moment you heard the news whether your human was guilty or innocent, didn't you? I don't mean Odelia, but her dad. Pets have a way of figuring this stuff out long before the cops do. Am I right or am I right?"

I felt a little ashamed to admit that I had no idea whether Tex was guilty or not.

"I think he wanted to kill Jaqlyn a little bit but he didn't know his own strength," said Dooley, subscribing to Brutus's theory.

"And what about you, Max? What do you think?" asked Jack. "Innocent or guilty?"

"I… I honestly don't know," I said. "I mean, can't a person be good and still do a bad thing?"

"You mean by accident? Sure. We all do stupid things from time to time. But deep down I think you know," he said now, tapping me on the chest. "Just look into your heart, Max. The truth is right there."

And with these words, the philosophical Schnauzer with the distinctly shaped hairy facial features trotted off in the direction of his human, to go and sit by the man's side.

Barney, when he became aware of his dog's presence, picked him up into his arms. Jack gave the man's face a lick and I found myself wondering about the dog's words.

Did I know, deep down inside, whether Tex was guilty or not? I closed my eyes for a moment, and tried to sense what I was feeling. But nothing came. As far as I could tell it really was a toss-up. Though I sure hoped Tex was innocent.

When I opened my eyes again I saw to my surprise that Dooley was looking pained. His face was screwed up and he looked as if he was going through a particularly painful and unsuccessful bowel movement.

"Dooley?" I asked. "Are you all right?"

He blinked and gave me a sad look. "I can't do it, Max. I can't make it work."

"You need to drink more," I said. "Drink plenty of liquids and everything will come out just fine."

"What will come out fine?"

"Well, your, um, stool."

"Oh, my stool is fine," he assured me. "It's just that I tried to do as Jack suggested and look into my heart but it doesn't work. All I see when I close my eyes is darkness. Did it work for you?"

"You don't literally have to look into your heart," I said with a laugh. "That's impossible. You have to look with your mind's eye."

"My mind has an eye?" he asked, surprised, and glanced up as if searching for this elusive eye.

I saw that in my attempt to explain a tough concept I'd made things even more complicated, so instead I said, "Just try to feel what's inside. Do you think that Tex is guilty or not?"

"Oh, but I already did that. Of course he's guilty. But the most important thing is that we shouldn't be too hard on him. After all, he killed Jaqlyn for all the right reasons."

I groaned. "There are no right reasons to justify murder, Dooley. None."

"There are if the person is really nasty, like Jaqlyn," he argued.

"No, there aren't."

"Are you sure? Not even a little?"

"Not even a teensy tiny bit."

It was obvious I'd given him some food for thought, for as

I scoured the street in search of other witnesses to the recent and tragic events, he lapsed into silence.

"All right," he said at length, "but I'm still going to keep liking Tex. No matter what he did."

"Fair enough," I said, and saw that a flock of birds were positioned in a nearby tree.

Time to bring out the inner diplomat.

29

*O*delia saw how Sarah Flunk walked away from Mayor Butterwick, closing the little notebook officers of the law consider part of their basic equipment, and decided to consult with her first.

Sarah, a red-haired and freckle-faced cop, seemed reluctant to talk to her, though, and Odelia could hardly blame her. The suspect in this case was, after all, Odelia's own father, and Sarah probably felt she wasn't exactly the most objective person in the world.

"Hey, Sarah," she said.

"Odelia," said Sarah, a little nervously.

"Um… Look, I know things aren't looking too good for my dad right now, but I'm hoping you'll keep an open mind and consider other possibilities."

"I'd say the chances of your father being the guilty party here are almost one hundred percent," said Sarah, making her position perfectly clear from the get-go.

"Oh, I know," said Odelia. "And frankly my first impulse was to believe he did it, too. But…"

Gran had joined her, and said, "Tex is innocent. And you can quote me on that."

Sarah rolled her eyes. "Really, Vesta, I think you better leave the police work to the police and stay out of this investigation. And that goes for you, too, Odelia. It's never a good idea for family members to insert themselves into an active investigation."

"Well, like it or not, I'm inserting myself to the hilt," said Vesta. "And now tell me, Officer Flunk, what have you found out so far? And don't even think about pooh-poohing me. You know I'm going to find out anyway by pestering my son. So start talking."

Sarah, who clearly felt she was in an impossible situation, decided to choose the path of least resistance. "Okay. So I talked to pretty much everyone present, and they all say the same thing: one minute Jaqlyn was there, and the next he was gone. No one saw where he went off to, though."

"Did you talk to the wife?" asked Gran. "Or the mistress?"

"Mistress?" asked Sarah with a frown. "What do you mean?"

"Oh, isn't it obvious? Jaqlyn was having an affair with Monica Chanting, and his wife found out about it. So obviously Francine had a strong motive to give her husband a whack across the adulterous noodle."

"I don't know..." Sarah began.

"Well, I do. Now go and do your job and talk to Francine. Ask her point blank about the affair and you'll see that I'm right."

Still frowning, Sarah walked off, scribbling something in her notebook. Probably a reminder to herself to steer clear of Gran and Odelia as much as humanly possible for the next foreseeable future.

"Clueless," said Gran. "That's what these people are.

Looks like it's up to us to clear your dad's name, honey. Come on."

Odelia followed her grandmother, a little trepidatious the old lady would lead her into more trouble than it was worth. Then again, wasn't justice for her dad worth all the trouble she could get in?

Mayor Charlene Butterwick stood texting on her phone when they joined her. She looked up, and seemed as displeased with their company as Sarah had been.

"I think you better go home," she suggested. "Nothing for you to do here now."

"We're not going home until we've caught Jaqlyn's killer," said Gran.

"But we already caught Jaqlyn's killer," said Charlene, a look of confusion on her face.

"Tex is innocent," said Gran. "So you better throw your mind back to the party and tell us when was the last time you saw Jaqlyn."

Charlene barked an incredulous laugh. "You're not seriously suggesting I killed Jaqlyn?"

"I'm seriously suggesting you reframe the situation and consider the possibility that someone other than my son-in-law killed the guy," said Gran. "Now talk, or I'm never voting for you again, and I'll tell all my friends to do the same thing."

Like any politician, Charlene lived by the grace of her voters, and the prospect of the entire senior citizen community of Hampton Cove voting for the other guy or gal at the next election quickly decided her. "Well, as far as I can tell Jaqlyn spent considerable time inside the house with Monica. At least that's what one of the waiters told me. He says that he saw Jaqlyn and Monica going up the stairs a little while before he went missing, and he says he could hear them arguing all the way down to the lobby."

"Arguing?" asked Odelia. "What were they arguing about?"

"The waiter says he couldn't hear their exact words, but it sounded serious."

"We need to talk to Monica," said Gran. "She'll be able to tell us."

"Look, this isn't right," said Charlene. "You shouldn't be doing this."

"We're the only ones standing between Tex and a miscarriage of justice, Charlene," said Gran. "So we are doing this, and you better get on board or else."

As they walked away, Odelia said, "Maybe you shouldn't go around antagonizing people like that, Gran. Charlene Butterwick isn't a bad person. In fact she's probably the best mayor this town has had in years."

"I know she's a fine mayor," said Gran. "But she's jumping to conclusions where Tex is concerned, and I simply can't have that. Now where is this Monica woman?"

They'd reached the house, where Monica had been treated for that scratch on her face, but as far as they could tell she was nowhere to be found. And then Odelia spotted her, seated on the same garden bench she and Mom had vacated earlier.

They quickly walked over and took a seat on either side of her. Monica looked startled by this ambush. "What do you want?" were the first words out of her mouth.

Maybe Gran was right, Odelia suddenly thought. No one would give them the time of day willingly, attributing some of the blame that now squarely fell on Tex to Tex's family. It was simple psychology, and Gran's crudeness cut right through that newly established bias.

"Tell us about your fight with Jaqlyn," said Gran. "We know you and him were having an affair so don't even bother denying."

"How do you…" Monica pressed her lips together. "Look, I didn't have anything to do with Jaqlyn's death, all right? So if you're trying to find some scapegoat so you can get your dad off, it's not going to work."

"I'm not trying to find a scapegoat," Odelia assured the woman. "I just want to know what happened, that's all."

Monica eyed her for a moment, then said, "Okay, fine. Jaqlyn and I were having an affair. Only for him it was just that, an affair. For me it was the beginning of something more. An actual relationship. I'd told him I wanted to divorce my husband and put what Jaqlyn and I had on a serious footing, and I expected the same from him. Only he was reluctant to tell his wife. So I said I'd tell her if he wasn't going to. He didn't like that."

"Was that what the fight was about?" asked Gran.

Monica nodded. "I said this was his last chance. If he didn't tell his wife today I was breaking up with him. He said he needed more time, and I said I'd waited long enough."

"How long had the affair been going on?" asked Odelia.

"Two months. I thought he was serious, but obviously he wasn't. At least not as serious as I was. So I broke up with him and walked out. I didn't see him after that. And then suddenly you told us you'd found him… dead." Tears welled up in her eyes and she took out a handkerchief to dab them away.

"You're sure you didn't take a swing at him yourself?" asked Gran.

Monica sat up straighter. "How can you even ask me that? Of course I didn't take a swing at him. I loved him. I would never—"

"You loved him but he didn't love you back. Is that how it was?"

"I think he did love me, in his own way."

"Obviously he didn't love you enough."

"No, obviously not," said Monica quietly. "Look, if you're looking for a person to blame, why don't you talk to Francine? She clearly knew about the affair, and was livid."

"Where did you go after you left Jaqlyn?" asked Odelia, feeling the need to be thorough now that her dad's future was at stake.

"I needed to cool off, so I went downstairs and sat in the living room for a while."

"Did anyone see you?"

"Yeah, plenty of people saw me. Waiters were passing to and from the kitchen all the time. Ask them. They can confirm I never moved from that spot until I felt composed enough to walk out and face the world again."

"She sounded plausible," said Gran as they left Monica and went in search of Francine Jones. "I don't think she did it."

"It'll be easy enough to verify her alibi," said Odelia. "Plenty of waitstaff were around."

They found Francine in front of the house, staring at the activity of cops and forensic people engaged in collecting evidence. A tent had been placed around Odelia's dad's car, which was now officially a crime scene.

"Francine, hi," said Odelia.

"Oh, God," said Francine in a low voice. She seemed as unhappy to see them as their other correspondents.

"Can we ask you a couple of questions?"

"No, you can't," said Francine brusquely. "You're not cops, and I don't want to talk to the daughter of the man who killed my husband," she snapped, and made to walk away.

But Gran grabbed her unceremoniously by the arm and said, "Not so fast, missy. First off, Tex didn't kill anyone—he's as much the victim here as your husband. And secondly, if I were a betting woman I'd pay good odds that you're the one who hit your husband over the head."

Francine uttered a startled yelp and tried to wrench her arm free. In vain. Vesta might look like a little old lady, but she had a surprisingly strong grip, and her bony fingers now dug deeply into the flesh of the widow's arm.

"Let go of me, you horrible woman!" Francine cried.

"Not before you tell me about the affair your husband was having with Monica Chanting. When did you find out—and don't lie to me."

"I–I've known for weeks," said Francine finally, and Gran let go. She rubbed the tender spot. "Jaqlyn left his phone at home one morning, and I noticed right away it wasn't his usual one. I didn't even know he'd gotten a second phone. When it started beeping with messages I couldn't resist the temptation to take a peek. They were all WhatsApp messages from that horrible woman."

"And I'll bet she wasn't the first one either."

Francine cast down her eyes. "No, she wasn't. Jaqlyn has always had trouble with fidelity, but I still loved him. He... he promised me the last time it happened that I was the only one for him. That these other women meant nothing. And I believed him."

"But this time was different." It was a statement, not a question.

"Yes, I think so. He seemed more serious. More invested in the relationship. And it lasted much longer than his usual flings."

"So you did what you had to do and confronted him."

"I was going to, yes, but Tex never gave me the chance," she said with an angry frown.

"Look, I can understand you think that way, but I can promise you that Tex didn't do this," said Gran, with conviction.

Francine seemed to waver. "But... if he didn't do it, then who did?"

"We already talked to Monica," said Odelia. "She has a solid alibi."

"How did you know I was thinking of her?"

"Isn't it obvious?" asked Gran. "Your husband wasn't prepared to commit to her, so she had every reason to be upset with him."

"Jaqlyn wasn't going to divorce me?" Francine asked feebly.

"No, I don't think he was. And I wonder why," said Gran, narrowing her eyes at the woman. She was like a dog with a bone, not letting go until she got what she wanted.

"I…" Francine shook herself, then said, "Look, I haven't told the police, but…" She gave Gran a searching look. "How sure are you that Tex didn't kill my husband?"

"One hundred percent. Tex is not a killer."

Francine nodded slowly. "I like Tex. He did me a big favor the other day. Well, the thing is… When we married, I was the one with the money. Or more precisely, my family."

"Was?"

"Yes, Jaqlyn managed to squander almost all of it. Gambled it away. My husband, Mrs. Muffin, had a serious gambling problem. It's the reason we had to move away from New Hampshire, and start a new life elsewhere. He made a good living over there, but even with the income he had he still managed to lose everything and most of my inheritance, too. He even lost our house and got in trouble with some local loan sharks. I… I'm afraid they may have found us and settled their score."

30

"*L*ook, Tex, there's no reason to hold out," said Chase. He and the father of the woman he loved were ensconced inside interview room number one, where they'd sat for the past hour, and frankly he was growing a little weary.

It is never pleasant for a police officer to be forced to handcuff and drag to prison the man whose daughter's hand one day he hopes to ask in marriage, but it's even worse when that man steadfastly refuses to tell him the truth. Not fair, Chase meant to say.

"I didn't do it," Tex said not for the first time. "I didn't like Jaqlyn, but I wasn't going to murder the man."

"You told your wife you were considering drastic measures. Radical solutions."

"I meant taking my music career to the next level! Taking the Singing Doctors national!"

"His body was found in the trunk of your car, Tex," Chase pointed out. "How else do you explain it got there unless you put it there?"

"I can't!"

"Look, isn't it possible you killed him in a fit of rage and then blanked it all out?"

"It's possible," Tex conceded. "I mean, theoretically such a scenario is certainly conceivable, but I don't have any recollection of blanking out."

"Well, you wouldn't, would you?"

"I doubt it," said Tex. "It's not as if I have a history of blanking out."

"How much did you have to drink?" asked Chase, deciding to try a different tack.

"One or two glasses maybe. They kept topping up, so it's hard to know for sure."

"And how well do you hold your liquor?"

Tex rolled his eyes. "You *know* how well I hold my liquor, Chase. Oh, come on, this is ridiculous! Why am I even here? You know as well as I do that I'm not a killer."

Chase sat back. "All I know is that you were overheard threatening Jaqlyn a couple of nights ago in a public meeting. Heck, you were even recorded." He placed his phone on the table and pressed play on a recording he'd found on the Soul Science website. They'd cleaned up the audio and Tex could clearly be seen and heard calling Jaqlyn a number of extremely opprobrious names.

Tex had the decency to look shamefaced. "Oh, God," he groaned, dragging his hands through his hair. "I said all that, didn't I?"

"And you meant it," Chase pointed out. "I was there, and so were a couple of dozen other witnesses. And they'll all gladly testify in court as to your state of mind and the animosity you harbored towards your future victim, Jaqlyn Jones."

"I *said* I didn't like him, didn't I? I'm not ashamed to admit it. But kill him? Never."

"Jaqlyn organized a concerted effort to drag your name

through the mud," said Chase, moving to the next point on the agenda. "He told several people you never finished medical school. That you got your degree from an online college located in Timbuktu and that you had to resort to dissecting vermin to get some practice after you were kicked out of college for plagiarism and exam fraud and generally being the worst student possible. He told some of your patients you were accused of involuntary manslaughter after you killed a patient through sheer incompetence but paid off certain people up top and managed to get the whole thing hushed up."

"What?!" Tex cried, looking flabbergasted.

"He also said you had a drinking problem, causing your hands to shake uncontrollably and that you had a history of messing up the dosages on your prescriptions. Oh, and he suggested you only employed Vesta because no one else would work with you, as you were prone to volcanic outbursts of rage and had at one point trashed your office." He looked up, and found that Tex sat staring at him, mouth agape.

"He said all that? No wonder my patients left me in droves."

"You're telling me you didn't know?"

"Of course! This is the first I'm hearing about this. I had noticed former patients of mine were avoiding me, crossing the street when they saw me coming. But I just figured they were embarrassed to meet me after switching doctors. If I'd known Jaqlyn was conducting this slanderous... this terrible... this *horrendous...*"

Chase leaned a little closer. "What would you have done if you found out?"

"I'd have beaned him!" Tex burst out, then realized what he'd said and clasped a hand before his mouth. "I... maybe I should talk to a lawyer," he finished sedately.

"Yeah, that's probably a good idea," Chase conceded.

🐦

*I*t's always a tough proposition for a cat to interview a bird. Birds, as a rule, don't like cats. It probably has something to do with the fact that birds have been on cats' menu for the past fifteen million years or so. And no matter how much I try to convince them that I'm not that kind of cat, my words are still met with a certain level of incredulity.

"Hi, there," I said now, employing the most genial and unthreatening tone in my arsenal.

The birds, all half a dozen of them, didn't respond. Birds tend to travel in packs, and these birds were no different.

"Hi birds," said Dooley, smiling a pleasant smile and also showcasing his best behavior. "Mind if we ask you a couple of questions, birds?"

But the birds were clearly not having any of this, and retained a dignified silence.

"The thing is, our human has recently been accused of murder," I explained, deciding to trudge ahead regardless, as a good detective does. "And we were wondering if you kind birds might have seen something. It happened right there," I said, indicating Tex's car, parked right across the street, though now obscured from view by that white tent.

"Is it true that birds like to eat worms?" asked Dooley, suddenly going off script.

"Dooley, now is not the time for this," I said. "Let's stick to our main topic."

"Yeah, but I figured since we're here anyway, and so are they…"

"Who cares about worms?"

"I care. I can't imagine how anyone could eat a worm, and

I just wondered if these nice birds could offer me an insider's view."

"Worms are very nutritious," suddenly one of the birds spoke. He was probably the leader, as he was the fattest bird of the lot. They were all sparrows, if I wasn't mistaken, and as a rule sparrows are pretty small, but this one was slightly less small than his ilk.

"That's what I keep hearing," said Dooley, pleased at the opportunity to worm information out of a bird. "But are they tasty? They don't look tasty. In fact they look yucky."

"Oh, they're very tasty," the bird confirmed. "And juicy, too."

"I wouldn't say all worms are juicy," another bird piped up. "Some of them are leathery. Like a shoe sole."

"Oh, yeah, tell me about it," said a third bird. "I had one of those last week. Terrible. Messed up my colon something nasty."

"So is it true you simply gobble them up whole, without chewing?" asked Dooley, fascinated by the turn the conversation had taken.

"Dooley!" I said.

"I'm curious!" he said.

"That's where the gizzard comes in," said the leader bird. "The secret is in the gizzard. But why do you ask? Are you interested in starting a worm-based diet?"

"Oh, no way," said Dooley, horrified by the mere suggestion. "But I find it fascinating to find out more about the eating habits of different species. You see, I watch a lot of the Discovery Chanel? And nothing beats a personal testimony like yours, Mr. Bird."

"Mrs. Bird," she corrected him.

"I'm sorry, Mrs. Bird," he said quickly.

"Now about this murder business," she said. "I'm sorry to say we only arrived at the scene after the whole thing was over, but we did see an altercation take place shortly before, one street over."

"An altercation?" I asked, perking up.

"Yes, between the man who now resides in the trunk of that there car and another man. They were speaking very loudly and motioning animatedly."

"Who was this other man?" I asked, hanging on this worm-eating creature's every word.

"I don't know his name, of course, but he was short."

"Tall," said another bird.

"Fat," piped up another.

"Skinny,'" determined yet another.

"Red-haired," said number five.

"Blond," opined bird six.

"Um…" I said. "So he was tall and short, fat and skinny, red-haired *and* blond?"

"Don't listen to them," said the leading sparrow. "He was short, squat and floppy-haired and for some reason he had the word Jason tattooed across his cheek."

I shared an excited look with Dooley.

"Jason Blowhard!" we both cried simultaneously.

31

*M*arge had gone down to the station house to see her husband, the jailbird. She encountered an immovable object in the shape of her own brother.

"No, you can't see him, Marge," said Alec. "He's a murder suspect, and the only one that can see him right now is his lawyer, which he doesn't have. Yet."

She planted her hands on her hips and gave her brother the look of a woman who wasn't going to be messed with. A woman who'd once discovered a stack of dirty magazines under her brother's bed and had proceeded to hand them to their mother and ask what the people in those magazines were doing. Alec had been grounded for the rest of the summer. 'I did it once, I can do it again,' her look seemed to say. Alec wilted.

"Alec Lip," she now said, her voice brooking no nonsense. "You listen to me and you listen good. You and Tex are practically brothers. In fact it's not an exaggeration to say that he's the brother you never had. You certainly love him like a brother, don't you?"

"Why, yes, I do, but—"

"And you're going to stand there and tell me he can't even receive a visit from his own wife—your sister? Shame on you."

"But—"

"Shame on you!"

Alec sighed. It was obvious he was thinking how hard it is to be a cop in times like these, when your own relatives start beaning people they don't like with baseball bats—aluminum or otherwise—and having wives that just happen to be your younger sister.

"I can't, Marge. If Mayor Butterwick found out she'd have my badge."

They were standing in the police precinct lobby, and Dolores Peltz, who combined desk sergeant duties with dispatch tasks, had pricked up her ears and was drinking in every single word of the back-and-forth between brother and sister. Free entertainment, she seemed to consider this minor showdown. Better than *Grey's Anatomy*.

"Who cares what Charlene Butterwick thinks! He's my husband and I want to see him. Now!"

"What's all this screaming and shouting?" asked Charlene Butterwick, walking in just then. "Hi, Marge. Chief. Dolores."

"Hi, Madam Mayor," said Dolores, eyes gleaming. Now this was going to be good, that gleam seemed to say. This was stuff Shonda Rhimes couldn't come up with if she tried.

"I want to see my husband and this man," said Marge, pointing an imperious finger at her brother, "is telling me I can't. Because he's afraid of you!" she added, redirecting that same accusing finger at the Mayor.

"It's fine, Alec," said the Mayor. "Let her see her husband."

"Madam Mayor?" asked Alec, surprised.

"I said let her through. I'm starting to think this whole case isn't as open and shut as I first thought. Did you know that Jaqlyn was having an affair with Monica Chanting?"

"Um…" said Alec, who clearly didn't.

"Or that Jaqlyn had huge gambling debts and practically had to flee loan shark enforcers in New Hampshire? Who may or may not have tracked him down here? And that Francine Jones had recently discovered his affair and wasn't too happy about it?"

"See?" said Marge triumphantly. "You arrested my husband without a second thought, and now you're going to have to let him go."

"It's not as simple as that, Marge," said the Mayor. "The victim's body was found in your husband's car, and he was overheard directing verbal threats at the man. There's dozens of witnesses, and the whole thing is on the internet for everyone to see. So…" She took off her glasses and carefully started polishing them with the hem of her blouse. "I think it's best if we hand this over to the state police and let them figure it out."

"The state police!" Alec cried. "But, Charlene!"

"He's your brother-in-law, Alec!" said Charlene. "And the lead detective in the case is dating the man's daughter. No, this case will be handled the way it should be handled. Which is by the book. I talked to the Assistant DA and he agrees this is all for the best. So you're off the case, and so is Chase, and as soon as we can arrange transport, Tex Poole will be taken to a holding facility, awaiting arraignment."

Marge, who'd hoped to find an ally in Charlene, saw the chances of a quick release of her husband suddenly being reduced to zero.

"You can't do this," she said. "You just told us there are other suspects."

"Which is exactly why I don't want sentimentality or family bonds or whatever to mess up this investigation. Now do you want to see your husband or not?"

"Yes, I do," said Marge, and followed the Mayor and Alec

inside, leaving Dolores to pick up her phone so she could gleefully start WhatsApping the news all around town.

Who needed a newspaper when they had Dolores?

Once inside, Marge was admitted into a small room, and moments later her husband was led in. He was still dressed in the same outfit he'd worn at the garden party, though he already looked a little worse for wear. There were smudges on his best Ralph Lauren polo shirt, and the collar was upturned, touching his left ear. He looked dazed and confused, but when he caught sight of Marge, his expression changed into a happy smile.

"Honey, you came all the way here!" he said, as if he were on Alcatraz and Marge had had to pay the ferryman to brave the churning and shark-infested seas to get there.

"Things aren't looking too good for you right now," said Marge, knowing she didn't have a lot of time allotted for this visit and wanting to convey as much information as she could. She was also aware curious eyes were watching them through the one-way mirror.

"Not too good is an understatement," said Tex, as they shared a warm hug. "I didn't do it, honey. At least not to my recollection. Chase seems to think I had a blackout or lapse of judgment and might not remember, so there's always that to take into account."

"It's all going to be fine," said Marge warmly, glad to see him. "Ma and Odelia have taken your case in hand and are interviewing witnesses and tracking down suspects."

"Your mother?" said Tex, clearly taken aback to find Vesta of all people in his corner.

"She's been amazing," Marge gushed. "You should see the way she bulldozes her way through a pack of reluctant witnesses. I think the world missed out on a great detective."

"How about Odelia?" Tex asked eagerly. "What does she think happened?"

Marge hesitated. She didn't want to tell her husband both she and Odelia actually thought he was guilty. Not great for his morale. Or those prying eyes watching them now. So instead she said, "Odelia has become a real champion for justice to prevail."

"Then everything will be all right," said Tex. "If Odelia is on the case, I don't have to worry about a thing. She'll catch the real killer." He gave her a sheepish look. "Unless I did do it, of course. In which case she's going to look really silly. And so is Vesta."

"Don't say things like that, Tex," Marge said, and darted a glance at that darned one-way mirror. "Don't say anything to incriminate yourself. Better yet, from now on don't say a single word without a lawyer."

"Can you get me one?" he asked, like a child asking for a lollypop.

"I'm working on it," she said. "But until then, don't talk to anyone."

"Not even Chase or your brother?"

Her expression hardened. "*Especially* them. These people are not your friends, Tex."

"But they're my family."

"No, they're not," she insisted. "The only family you've got is me and Odelia and my mother. My brother and Chase are dead to us from now on. You understand? *Dead.*"

And to make sure her words registered, she directed a pointed look at that mirror.

She could almost hear the glugging sound her brother made as he gulped at her harsh words and choked on his fat forked tongue.

For Kingman this was the first time he was playing detective, officially sanctioned by Max himself, Hampton Cove's premier feline sleuth. And he had to admit it was a lot tougher than he'd anticipated.

He'd thought that as soon as he started on his quest for clues, the little suckers would start filing in and report for duty, one after the other.

Instead, he discovered that the problem wasn't a dearth of clues but an abundance! Clue after clue came flying at him and he had a hard time distinguishing between the really vital ones and the ones that could safely be called duds and were to be discarded.

For instance smack out of the gate he saw that a waiter was eating his own hors d'oeuvres, furtively glancing around as he did. Suspicious, Kingman felt. Portentous, even. Could this man be the killer? Very likely, Kingman felt. But then he saw a second waiter, a female one this time, smoking a cigarette and talking into her phone.

"I know I shouldn't have done it, Dad, but he made me," she was saying.

Kingman's heart skipped a couple of beats. Here it was: a real confession! Straight from the horse's mouth—or in this case the killer's!

"What was I supposed to do, Dad? The man simply left me no choice!"

Kingman was listening with bated breath, his eyes having gone a little pop-eyed. He had to tell Max. He had to tell him to call off the hunt, for Kingman had solved the case!

"Okay, so next time I'll tell Mario I already made other arrangements. No, I'm not going to tell him I was supposed to head down to Southampton to visit Gran this weekend." She smiled. "If only he paid better, I wouldn't mind so much, but the man is the stingiest caterer I know."

Kingman could almost hear the sound of a record scratch, and gave the waitress in question an offended look. Not fair, he felt. Making him think she was the killer when all the while she was talking about such mundane matters as having to work the weekend.

Still, Kingman wasn't the kind of cat who gave up without a fight, and so he resumed his sleuthing. He quickly found himself searching out the company of his own human, Wilbur Vickery, who stood conferring with Father Reilly. Both men were standing right next to the drinks table and were helping themselves to the late Jaqlyn Jones's liquor stash, casually refilling their glasses without the inconvenience of an officiating waiter. Then again, Father Reilly was probably used to serving himself, and so was Wilbur.

"I don't believe for one second that Tex killed Jaqlyn," said Wilbur. "I've known Tex for years, and the guy just doesn't have it in him to commit murder. It takes a special kind of person to kill a man in cold blood, and believe you me, Tex Poole is not that person."

"Oh, I think you're absolutely right, Wilbur," said the

priest, slurring his words a little. "But I also think you're wrong."

"How do you figure that?" asked Wilbur, whose eyes were distinctly unfocused. "I mean, he either did it or he didn't do it, if you see what I mean."

"He did it... and he didn't do it," Father Reilly specified, continuing to fog the issue. "Why don't I explain myself?"

"Please do, father."

"Tex Poole was a mere instrument of the devil, my dear Wilbur. He didn't want to kill Jaqlyn, but the devil took possession and made him raise his hand against a fellow man."

"The devil, eh? Nasty piece of work, that one," Wilbur concurred.

"He most certainly is. And wily. Extremely wily. And I think it's plain to see who the real culprit is in this case." He dropped his voice to a whisper, and both Wilbur and Kingman leaned in. "Omar Carter."

"Omar Carter?" asked Wilbur, as if hearing that name for the first time.

"Omar Carter," Father Reilly confirmed.

"Oh, Omar Carter!" said Wilbur.

"One and the same. He and Jaqlyn Jones must have fallen out, and so Omar decided to get rid of him—shut him up before he could spill all of Omar's dirty little secrets."

"So..." Wilbur swayed a little, like a willow in the breeze. "So what you're saying..."

"What I'm saying is that Omar took possession of poor Tex and used him like a tool."

"Tex Poole, Omar's tool..."

"Satan never leaves home without donning a disguise, my dear Wilbur. In this case he ever so cunningly disguised himself as the leader of a new cult named Soul Science."

Wilbur took a long and galvanizing gulp from his glass.

Things were getting a little complicated for him. "So... Omar is Satan, who killed Jaqlyn because... why, exactly?"

"Because Jaqlyn had decided to leave the fold. Never leave the fold, Wilbur!"

"Never leave the fold," Wilbur echoed.

"Leave the fold and die."

"But I don't want to die," Wilbur intimated.

Kingman's head was swimming. So now Omar was the killer? But how? And why? This was getting trickier and trickier. And he now wished he had one of those notebooks detectives like to carry on their person. If he didn't write down this abundance of clues and hypotheses he was likely to forget one or two of the more spectacular ones.

He moved on from his master and his master's cohort, and decided to take a little break to gather his thoughts and draw some preliminary conclusions. In detective shows the lead detective always gets a brainwave at some point, and tells himself, 'But of course! Why didn't I see this sooner!' This invariably comes on the heels of that crucial moment of personal crisis when he frowns to himself in utter confusion and mutters to his loyal but goofy sidekick, 'There's something I'm not seeing. Something I missed...'

Kingman felt he was at the latter stage: he was missing something. He sincerely hoped the final stage would soon be upon him: the lightbulb stage.

And he was sitting and thinking when two men approached. They were both heavyset, with the kind of square and pockmarked faces only a mother could love.

"You shouldn't have done it, Mike," said one of the men, addressing his friend.

"How could I have known he was gonna drop dead on us?" said the other reasonably.

"Just don't tell Francine, will you? She'll never forgive us."

"She should thank us."

"You know what she's like. Even though the guy was scum, she still stood by him."

"Something I'll never understand."

"Well, she's finally rid of him."

"And good riddance, too."

Suddenly a woman came walking up, and smiled at the sight of the twosome. "Mike and Kenny—you guys still here? I thought you left already."

"We couldn't leave now, Francine," said the man named Mike. "Leaving you to cope with the cops all by yourself? Never."

"Are the police still out there?" asked Kenny.

Francine nodded, her smile disappearing. "They just took away Jaqlyn's... body." She stifled a sob, and Mike took her into a hug, quickly joined by Kenny.

"It's gonna be all right," said Mike a little gruffly. "Your big brothers are here for you."

"What would I do without you guys?" said Francine, sniffling.

"That's what family is for, little sis," said Kenny.

Kingman had a hard time controlling the wealth of emotions welling up in his bosom.

But of course! Why hadn't he seen it sooner?! Francine's two brothers had killed Jaqlyn to protect their sister from the man's shenanigans! Eureka! He'd solved the case!

*H*arriet was a cat with a mission. She had the feeling she'd made a complete fool of herself with the Soul Science thing, both in the eyes of her housemates and her friends, and she now felt the strong urge to redeem herself by solving this particular crime.

"We have to find who did it, Brutus," she said therefore. "It's very important to me."

"And we will, twinkle toes," her partner in life and sleuthing said.

They'd been roaming Jaqlyn and Francine Jones's backyard for a while now, but so far no clues had fallen into their laps, so to speak.

"I can't go back to Odelia empty-handed, sugar bear," she said, continuing to develop her theme. "So promise me we won't go home until we've caught the killer, sweetums."

"We won't go home until we catch the killer, baby cakes," said Brutus, though not wholeheartedly, she felt.

It wasn't merely her reputation that was at stake here, but also the future of Tex, that wonderful human who'd selflessly taken care of them for all those years. After all, if it hadn't been for Tex, none of them would have a home to begin with. It was Tex, with his quiet support and kindhearted generosity, who had made it possible for Odelia and Marge and Vesta to adopt no less than four cats in the first place, and offer them the kind of life to which they'd now become accustomed.

And as Harriet let her eyes dart across the faces of the dozens of people still roaming about, and still filling their bellies with the dead man's food and drink, she suddenly caught sight of a familiar face and grumbled, "Stop me before I do something to that cat, Brutus. Stop me now," she repeated when Brutus made no attempts to stop her now.

Shanille had caught sight of her, too, and gave her the kind of supercilious look she'd perfected since rising through the ranks of Master Sharif's feline following.

"Harriet," Shanille said coldly as they passed each other by.

"Shanille," said Harriet, adopting an equally icy tone.

"Nice to see you."

"Likewise."

After a final frosty glance, they both sailed on.

"Stop you from doing what, cuddle cakes?" asked Brutus, late to the party as usual.

"Oh, Brutus," Harriet sighed, and headed straight for the food table. She was in urgent need of a pick-me-up, and besides, a sleuth was like a shark: they never stopped moving.

And it was as she neared the refreshments table that she saw that the waiters, still out in full force in spite of the recent tragedy, had placed the remnants of what had once been a fish dish on the ground behind the table. She smiled, momentarily forgetting all about clues and killers, and took a tentative nibble. Approving of the offered treat, she settled down to do some real damage, quickly joined by Brutus, happy for this respite.

Next to them, two humans had taken up position, and were talking quietly amongst themselves. They were an older man with a gray buzz cut and a red and veiny bulbous nose, and a young woman with a blond bob, cornflower blue eyes and a pretty face.

"We should never have come here, Daddy," said the young woman. "We should have simply said no."

"It's all right, Jenny," said her father. "Nobody knows, and that's how it's gonna stay. You didn't tell the police, did you?"

"Not a word," Jenny assured him.

Harriet, even though distracted by the fish, which was, indeed, excellent, still had the presence of mind to turn her ears like antennae and drink in every word of the conversation.

"You should never have approached him, Daddy. And now look what happened."

"So I lost my temper—can you blame me? He practically killed you, honey. If we hadn't taken you to the hospital you would have died, and all because of the man's incompetence."

"You still didn't have to attack him," said Jenny. "If the police find out you'll be in big trouble, Daddy."

"The police aren't going to find out. I made sure there were no witnesses, and Jaqlyn sure as heck isn't going to tell anyone now. He's dead."

"Oh, Daddy," said the girl. "I hope you're right. I can't lose you now."

"And you won't. I promise."

They walked off, and Harriet gave her boyfriend an excited prod. "Did you hear that?"

"Hear what?" asked Brutus, munching on a piece of fish, his eyes closed with relish.

"Don't tell me you didn't hear Jenny and her dad!"

"Jenny who?"

"Oh, Brutus—I just solved Jaqlyn's murder and you didn't even pay attention!"

"I'm paying attention now, my sweet love sponge," he said, opening his eyes and glancing around. "So who is this Jenny person?"

Under normal circumstances Harriet would have been displeased that her boyfriend paid so little attention to her, or in this case to whatever she paid attention to, but these weren't normal circumstances so she decided to let it go.

"Didn't you hear what I just said? I solved Jaqlyn's murder! Me!"

"Congratulations, buttercup!" said Brutus, then dug in for more fish.

a big meeting had been called, and all the usual suspects were present and accounted for: Odelia, who'd called the meeting. Gran, who acted as co-chair. Marge, and of course myself, Dooley, Harriet and Brutus. We even had a guest star in the form of Kingman, who, judging from the way he kept directing a self-satisfied smirk at me, had exciting news to impart.

Absent were Tex, who had been taken away in the paddy wagon, Chase, who had been driving the paddy wagon, and Uncle Alec, who owned the paddy wagon and who was, as we speak, presumably tying Tex to the police station torture rack preparatory to applying gentle pressure until the man cracked under the strain and confessed all.

The location of the meeting was Odelia's place, and all five cats were comfortably ensconced on the couch while Marge and Gran were seated on chairs, with Odelia standing in front of her whiteboard, waving a black marker and writing down the names of potential suspects and their possible motives.

In other words, a classic set-up. Hercule Poirot would

have nodded approvingly, and so would Sherlock Holmes, Perry Mason and Nero Wolf, had any of them been present.

"Francine Jones," Odelia said, jotting down the name of Jaqlyn's widow. "She had recently discovered that her husband was having an affair with Monica Chanting."

"Monica Chanting herself," said Gran. "Who wanted the affair to blossom into a marriage but found that Jaqlyn was reluctant to tell his wife and file for divorce."

"How about Monica's husband Garvin Chanting?" Marge suggested. "He could have found out about his wife's affair and decided to take matters into his hands."

Odelia dutifully wrote down the name of Monica's husband and his motive.

"Okay, so next we have Barney Sowman, the neighbor whose tires had been slashed by Jaqlyn, and who was involved in a dispute with the man over an access road."

"Barney definitely had his own ideas about the murder," I said, and reported Barney's suggestions for a potential murder weapon. It made quite an impact on my audience, and Odelia added a red asterisk next to Barney's name, to indicate he was a promising suspect.

"Other suggestions?" she asked now, glancing around.

Just then, the door opened and two men walked in. Reading from left to right they were none other than Chase and Uncle Alec.

Instantly, Marge was on her feet. "Oh, no!" she cried, shaking her head vehemently. "You two aren't welcome here anymore. Out! Both of you—out! Traitors!"

"But, Marge!" said Uncle Alec, clearly taken aback.

"*You* arrested my husband," said Marge, pointing an accusing finger at Chase, who looked stricken and a little scared of the woman, "and *you* handed him over to the state police without batting an eye," she added, turning that same finger on her brother, who'd gone a little white around the nostrils all of a sudden. "You're both dead to me. *Dead!*"

"Mom," said Odelia, "they were just doing their jobs. You can hardly blame them."

"I do blame them. I blame them for robbing a good man of his freedom over some unfounded suspicions."

"He had a body stashed in the trunk of his car!" Alec cried.

"So? That's still no reason to arrest him."

"Marge, settle down," said Gran, adopting a harsh tone. "You're acting like an idiot."

"Oh, *I'm* acting like an idiot, am I? *They're* the ones who are the idiots, and they'll feel pretty stupid when they discover that Tex is innocent. And now get out of my house!"

"It's not your house," Gran pointed out.

"I don't care! Out of my sight!"

"Marge Lip!" Gran bellowed suddenly, causing Marge to jump. "Shut up and sit down!"

"But—"

"Now!"

"Yes, Ma," Marge muttered, and did as she was told.

"We're in the middle of a family crisis and this is not the time to lose your head. We all need to work together to get Tex off the hook, and you're not helping."

"Yes, Ma," said Marge dutifully.

"Chase and Alec were only doing their duty. When you're a cop and you find a dead body in the trunk of a car, you arrest the guy who owns the car, it's that simple. If Chase hadn't arrested Tex, someone else would have, and Chase would have had a lot to answer for, maybe even lost his job. And the same goes for Alec. Now please let's dispense with the drama and focus on finding the real killer. Chase—take a seat. You, too, Alec. Odelia, get on with it. We haven't got all day."

Everyone settled down, and Odelia took up position in front of her whiteboard again. In deference to the latecomers, she quickly reiterated the list of suspects she'd compiled so far: Francine Jones, Monica Chanting, Garvin Chanting and Barney Sowman.

"Max, you have the floor," she said now. "What did you find out so far?"

"Well, apart from Barney's eagerness to select a suitable murder weapon to dispense with annoying neighbors, the birds in a nearby tree said they saw Jason Blowhard and Jaqlyn Jones have a big fight on the next street shortly before Jaqlyn's murder."

"Jason Blowhard," Odelia said, writing down the name on the board, and translated my words for the non-cat-speaking part of the group.

"We also discovered that some worms are not very juicy," said Dooley helpfully. "Some are really chewy and tough to digest. But birds have a gizzard and so that helps."

Odelia stared at him for a moment, then said, "Thank you, Dooley. Moving on…"

Harriet cleared her throat. I'd noticed she looked pleased as punch, and based on her next words she had every right to be.

"Brutus and I overheard a conversation between a man and a woman. The woman is called Jenny and the man is her father. And I think it's pretty obvious she's the girl who was misdiagnosed by Jaqlyn and later on was discovered to be suffering from a brain tumor. And guess what? He killed Jaqlyn! He confessed! Isn't that right, Brutus?"

"Uh-huh," said Brutus, not exactly providing a ringing endorsement.

"Wow," said Gran. "Good work, Harriet and Brutus. Write that down, Odelia."

But Odelia didn't need her grandmother's instructions.

She was already writing down 'Jenny's father—revenge,' before translating Harriet's words for the others.

"Kingman?" asked Odelia. "You wanted to share something?"

"Oh, boy, do I have something to share!" Kingman cried, thumping his chest. "I know who did it and it wasn't Jenny's dad. Francine's brothers Mike and Kenny were at the party, and they decided to have a chat with Jaqlyn about the way he was treating their little sister. Things got out of hand and they beat him to death. I heard it from their own lips!"

The moment Odelia translated Kingman's bombshell revelation, the room erupted into an excited clamor. Now this was the goods! The only one who wasn't impressed was Harriet. "I still think Jenny's dad did it," she intimated stubbornly. "Isn't that right, Brutus?"

"Oh, sure," said Brutus. "Jenny's dad—no doubt about it."

"So Mike and Kenny," said Odelia, writing on her board. "We need to talk to them as soon as possible."

"Well done, Kingman," said Gran, patting the cat on the head. "Good job."

"Thanks," said Kingman. "Some people would call it beginner's luck, but I think I'm simply a natural. It's all in being discerning when gathering clues. Knowing which ones to keep and which ones to toss. For instance Father Reilly kept babbling on about how Master Omar was the one that did it, by possessing Tex and using his body like a puppet and making him do his bidding. But that's just a lot of horse manure if you ask me."

Odelia stared at him. "Father Reilly thinks Master Omar did it? But why?"

"Well, Father Reilly claims Jaqlyn was about to leave the fold and spill all of Master Omar's secrets, and Omar couldn't have that, so he shut Jaqlyn up. Permanently."

Odelia nodded, and wrote down Master Omar's name

between brackets, just to be on the safe side. Odelia is nothing if not diligent.

"Okay, so we have plenty of suspects and plenty of alibis to check out," she said now. "Does anyone want to add anything at this point? Any comments, thoughts, insights?"

Uncle Alec tentatively raised his hand, braving a scathing look from his sister. "Um... the state police have taken over the investigation, so officially Chase and I are both off the case. Which means we can't interview suspects, or even come near them."

"Yeah, they don't trust us," said Chase. "Being Tex's relatives and all."

"Well, that's fine," said Gran. "It just means we'll have to clear Tex's name ourselves. I suggest we divvy up the suspects and try and track them down. We already talked to Monica and Francine, and Monica has a solid alibi, so we can scratch her off the list."

"I talked to Barney," said Uncle Alec. "And my gut tells me he didn't do it."

"Your gut also told you to arrest my husband," said Marge pointedly.

"Oh, Marge, please give it a rest," said Gran. "So no Barney?"

"Barney's dog Jack didn't think he did it either," I said. "He looked into his master's heart and saw that it was pure as gold."

"I tried to look into my heart but I couldn't see a thing," Dooley shared.

"Right," said Odelia, scratching off Barney's name as well as Monica's. "About Francine... I don't think she did it either. We talked to her and she didn't strike me as a cold-blooded murderess." She put the woman's name between brackets. "So that leaves us with Jason Blowhard, Jenny's dad, and Francine's brothers Mike and Kenny." She underlined the names of Jenny's dad and Francine's brothers. "These look promising."

"And let's not forget about the loan sharks," said Uncle Alec. "Jaqlyn owed them a lot of money and Charlene thinks they may have followed him here."

"No witness reports to support that theory, though," Chase added.

"Still worth checking out," Gran decided. "Write it down, Odelia."

"Loan sharks," Odelia said, adding this peculiar fauna to her impressive list.

"I'll talk to Jenny's dad," said Marge. "I know Nick pretty well. I'm sure he'll talk to me, especially with Tex being hung out to dry for a murder he didn't commit."

"And maybe we can go and have a chat with Francine's brothers," Gran suggested to her granddaughter.

"What do you want me to do?" asked Chase. "I can't talk to witnesses but there must be something I can do."

"You're sitting this one out, Kingsley," said Marge sternly. "You're in the doghouse now. And I suggest you stay there and don't move until I decide whether I'll forgive you."

"Yes, ma'am," said Chase, and Odelia gave him a wink, which cheered him up considerably.

"What can we do?" I asked.

"You can join us when we interview Francine's brothers," said Odelia. "And Harriet and Brutus can join Mom when she talks to Jenny and her dad."

"What about me?" asked Kingman. "I'm on fire here. So please use me, Miss Odelia."

Odelia smiled at this. "Why don't you go and talk to Shanille and try to pump her for information on Father Reilly and his particular views on Master Omar?"

"But... I thought that was a dead end?" said Kingman.

"A good detective follows up on every single lead," she

said, giving him a tickle behind the ears. "No matter how inconsequential, you never know what they might yield."

"Okay, Miss Odelia!" said Kingman, well pleased with these nuggets of wisdom rolling from the detective's lips. "I'll pump Shanille like she's never been pumped before!"

"Um, go easy on her, will you?" said Gran. "If I know Shanille she might not like all of this... pumping. Delicacy and tact go a long way—take it from a tactful person like me."

All the humans present laughed at this, and Gran frowned. "What? What did I say?"

Just then, Odelia's phone tinkled and she picked up with a cheerful, "Odelia Poole speaking." She then glanced at the others present. "Yes, I will hold for Master Omar."

A hush descended on the room, and Odelia switched her phone to speaker mode.

"Hi, Odelia," said Omar. "This is Omar speaking. I heard about what happened this afternoon and I've decided to call an extra meeting tonight to deal with the aftermath of Jaqlyn's death. I wanted to invite you and your family personally, considering your father seems to be embroiled in this terrible tragedy as well."

"A special meeting?" asked Odelia.

"We're not going!" Gran loud-whispered.

"Oh, hi there, Vesta," said Omar. "You're invited too, of course. Francine Jones is also coming, her brothers Mike and Kenny, Monica Chanting and her husband Garvin, Barney Sowman, Jenny and Nick Parker and, um, I have a feeling I'm forgetting someone..."

Odelia's eyes went wide when she realized Omar had just listed all of our suspects.

"I think it will be beneficial to thresh this thing out once and for all, don't you agree?" Omar continued. "And what better way to heal a lot of broken hearts and pain than by bringing the entire community together to commemorate that unfortunate Jaqlyn?"

"Um, I guess," said Odelia, not entirely convinced. "So... this is a private meeting?"

"Yes, just the people I've mentioned and your family."

"Are you going to film the whole thing like you always do?" asked Gran, leaning into her granddaughter's phone and speaking with a touch of rancor.

Omar chuckled. "No, not this time, Vesta. This will be just us. So how about it?"

Odelia seemed to make up her mind. "We'll be there," she said.

"Good. See you later."

"Is Scarlett coming?" asked Gran, but Omar had already disconnected. "If I see Scarlett I'm out of there," she announced. "Like a flash."

"Don't be an idiot, Ma," said Marge. "We're in the middle of a family crisis and this is not the time to lose your head. So let's dispense with the drama, shall we?"

Gran grumbled something that sounded a lot like, "Miss Smartypants," but shut up.

"I hope Shanille won't be there," said Harriet. "If I see Shanille I'm out of there like a flash." But when Marge raised an eyebrow in her direction she, too, shut up.

This was not the time for frail egos to thump their chests and bay like a pack of wild dogs. Now was the time to come together and save Tex from his terrible predicament.

3 5

*O*nce again we took the road down to Tavern Street to attend one of Master Omar's meetings, only this time there weren't as many people as before. The bodyguards were still there, scrutinizing us closely, presumably for signs of concealed weapons or bad intentions, but once we were admitted to the building the usual buzz of activity was conspicuously absent. Instead we were immediately led into the main hall, where chairs had been placed in a circle. Omar was there, officiating the proceedings, and greeting us with warmth and genuine affection, and a few participants had already taken a seat: Jason Blowhard, Francine Jones and two burly men I assumed were her brothers Mike and Kenny, Monica Chanting and husband and... Mayor Butterwick and Father Reilly!

"What are you doing here?" asked Gran as she took a seat next to the priest.

"I was invited," said Father Reilly. "I may not always see eye to eye with the man, but when I'm cordially invited I find it rude to refuse to grace a meeting with my presence."

"I have no idea why he invited us," said Charlene, "but I have to confess I'm curious."

"Welcome, welcome, one and all," said Omar, as he gestured for everyone to take their seats. "We're only waiting for the Parkers and Mr. Sowman and we're complete."

"So what's the idea?" asked Alec, who'd never been a big fan of the church leader.

"After the tragic events of this afternoon, I think we should all take a moment to reflect on the fleeting nature of life," said Omar, wreathing his face in mournful frowns. "Plus, I'd like to find out who killed my friend Jaqlyn, and I can think of no better way than bringing everyone together and seeing if we can't figure this out together."

Outside of the circle of humans, a second circle had been organized, only this one not consisting of chairs but cushions placed on the floor. And here Master Sharif was officiating, and welcoming us to this peculiar and unusual gathering. Immediately I saw that Shanille was also there, in fact seated to Sharif's immediate left, as if already having risen through the ranks to the highest position available.

"I'm out of here," Harriet announced, and started walking away.

"Harriet, please take a seat!" Sharif caroled, his voice echoing through the room.

Harriet halted in her tracks. "And why would I do that?" she asked, half-turning.

"Shanille has a confession to make, haven't you, Shanille?" said Sharif.

Shanille didn't speak. She merely looked uneasy. "No, I haven't," she finally said.

"Shanille wants you to know she regrets the harsh words directed at you," said Sharif.

"No, I don't," Shanille muttered.

"Yes, she does. And she wants you to know how important it is for her to make amends. Please shake paws with Harriet, Shanille. Be the bigger cat."

Shanille looked as if she'd much rather do anything than shake paws with Harriet, but her master's voice decided her. So it was with visible reluctance that she got up and walked over to Harriet. She held up her paw. "I'm sorry," she mumbled, almost inaudibly.

"What was that?" asked Sharif. "I didn't catch it."

"I said I'm sorry," said Shanille, louder this time.

Harriet eyed her with marked disdain, gave the other cat's paw a slight slap, then both cats turned their backs and stalked off in opposite directions and took their seats.

"How touching," said Dooley. "Friends once more."

"I doubt it," said Brutus, and hurried to take a seat next to his mate, while Dooley and I made ourselves comfortable, and so did Kingman, our special guest this evening.

The final guests arrived in the form of Jenny Parker and her dad Nick, and Jaqlyn's neighbor Barney, and the door of the room was closed, the two guards taking position in front of it, and then the lights were turned down a notch, creating a special atmosphere.

"My friends, most welcome to my home," said Omar, spreading his arms. "First off, I have a confession to make."

"This should be good," Kingman said.

"When I returned to Hampton Cove, where I grew up, I was just an ordinary guy with a big dream. I'd made my fortune on Wall Street for the past sixteen years, and had firsthand experienced the emptiness of a life devoted to the amassing of material wealth. Oh, I had all the accouterments of success: the Lambo, the Manhattan condo, the glamorous model girlfriend, but even though my nights were spent with the in-crowd frequenting fancy restaurants and cool clubs, I felt empty inside. Unhappy. It took almost getting killed in a car crash to realize my life wasn't going in the right direction."

"I think I've seen this movie, Max," said Dooley. "Wasn't Nicolas Cage in it?"

"He was," I confirmed, remembering the movie *The Family Man* with fondness. Though in that particular movie it took meeting an angel for Nic to change his ways.

"So while convalescing I picked up a Bible the hospital pastor had been so thoughtful to gift me, and started thumbing through the thing. It wasn't the kind of reading I was used to. Not exactly Grisham or Patterson. Still, I became intrigued, and over the course of the next couple of weeks I decided to turn my life around. Focus on feeding my soul, instead of my avarice. Spreading happiness instead of ROI. And Soul Science was born."

"A cult," Father Reilly grumbled.

"A way to share my newfound wisdom," Omar countered. "I never wanted to launch a new religion, or a cult, or whatever. I simply wanted to bring people together and show them there's more to life than simply collecting a bunch of material possessions."

"You collected followers instead," said the priest. "Isn't that the same thing?"

"I admit I got carried away a little in my zeal to spread the word," said Omar. "And for that I apologize. I don't want to be a guru, or a new pope or modern prophet. All I want is to come together with a group of likeminded people and talk about our experience."

"Well, you sure helped me," said Jason. "No offense, Father Reilly, but he did."

"And I'm glad for that, Jason," said Omar. "But I see now that in setting up Soul Science I've created a monster. So I'm hereby officially disbanding the organization, and announcing that Soul Science is no more."

His surprise announcement was met with gasps of shock.

"Jaqlyn's death has made me think, and this is what I've come up with. People are always looking for a leader to follow, and I admit I was honored and touched when they decided to follow me. Me, a former investment banker! Anyway, I think it's time to stop this nonsense. Which brings me to my second point." He glanced around the room, his eyes darting from face to face. "Someone killed Jaqlyn, and his killer is in our midst."

"But I thought Tex Poole killed Jaqlyn?" asked Barney, clearly much surprised. "Using an aluminum baseball bat or billy club? Or it could have been a nice steel hammer…"

"Tex is innocent," said Omar. "I have it on good authority that the person who is really responsible tried to make it look as if Tex killed Jaqlyn, and they did a pretty good job."

"What are you saying?" asked Charlene. "That you know who really killed Jaqlyn?"

"Yes," said Omar. "I know who killed Jaqlyn."

This time there was a stunned silence, as people stared at the former guru.

"But I think it's important that the person who did it comes forward and tells you himself what happened." Omar directed a knowing look at one of those present and said, in a kindly tone, "So how about it? Are you going to tell them or do you want me to do it?"

"What's going on, Max?" asked Dooley.

"I think Omar has just revealed who Jaqlyn's killer is," I said.

"But... isn't Odelia supposed to do that? She's the detective, isn't she?"

"Well, it looks like things have taken a slightly different turn this time," I said.

"Twists and turns," Kingman whispered. "All of the books Wilbur likes to read got them. He says he can't read a book that isn't filled to the rim with twists and turns."

Well, this was a twist, all right. One of those things you don't see coming until they hit you in the snoot. Or the patootie.

Jason Blowhard, for it was he who'd been singled out by Omar, opened and closed his mouth a couple of times. It was obvious he hadn't seen this one coming either. He glanced longingly to the door, but the two sturdily-built bodyguards standing sentry quickly made him see that there was no escape possible.

"I have no idea what you're talking about," he said now, in

an unconvincing attempt at bluster. "He's gone mad," he declared to the others present. "The man has gone completely screwy! That's what happens when you go around declaring that you're some kind of god in human shape. It starts to mess up your brain."

"I never said I was a god in human shape," said Omar, leaning back. "All I ever wanted was to talk about the soul, and you guys started assuming stuff. Calling me a god and saying that Soul Science was a new religion and yadda yadda yadda. You did that."

"Did you kill Jaqlyn, Jason?" asked Uncle Alec, assuming his role as chief of police.

"No, sir," said Jason, shaking his head decidedly. "No, sir, I did not. Tex Poole did."

"Oh, nonsense," said Gran. "Tex wouldn't hurt a fly. When I told him the other day to rid my roses of greenfly he told me the poor creatures had a right to live as much as the next garden pest. The man is a softie. And I should know. He married my daughter twenty-five years ago and I've come to love him like a son ever since. And if any of you dare tell him that I'll hunt you all down and kill you like the rats you are," she warned.

"I thought you killed Jaqlyn," said Chase, gesturing to Jenny's dad. "For almost killing your daughter."

"I did have a word with the guy," Jenny's dad acknowledged, "and I admit I had to restrain myself from landing a punch in his no-good incompetent face, but in the end I couldn't do it. My little girl wouldn't have liked her dad to get into trouble like that."

"But you did give him a piece of your mind, didn't you, Dad?" said Jenny proudly.

"Oh, you bet I did," said Nick Parker. "He paled beneath his tan, the horrible ass."

If Francine Jones was hurt by these epithets being hurled

at her dead husband, she didn't show it. Instead, she said, "I could have killed him myself, but I didn't. I thought about it for a moment, but I figured he wasn't worth going to prison for."

"I'm sorry I did that to you, Francine," said Monica, seated next to her, and held out her hand. After a moment's hesitation, Francine took it.

"And I'm sorry I scratched you," she said.

"I deserved it," said Monica. "I was a fool, falling for the guy, but it took me until now to realize it."

"And I was a fool to stay married to him for all these years, even after he gambled away my inheritance, and cheated on me practically the entire time we were married."

"He was scum," said her brother Kenny. "Well, he was, sis," he said emphatically when she gave him a look. "The world is better off without him. *You're* better off without him."

"I just wish I'd squeezed harder when I had my hands around his neck," his brother Mike grumbled.

"You didn't," said Francine, wide-eyed.

"Oh, yes, I did. I told him in no uncertain terms what I thought of him, and he squealed like a pig when I lifted him clear off the floor."

"So… did you kill him?" asked Odelia.

"No, I didn't," said Mike. "I finally let him go, after he promised me he was going to sign the divorce papers the moment they arrived, which I told him wouldn't be long."

"I could have killed him," said Barney Sowman now. "A nice big whack across the occipital bone with an aluminum bat would have done the trick. Or just your plain household hammer, of course," he allowed, for the sake of argument.

"But you didn't?" asked Uncle Alec.

"Nope, I didn't. Tex beat me to it," he said with a touch of regret. "Literally. Though in all honesty I probably wouldn't have gone through with it. I think when push comes to shove

I don't have it in me to go around murdering people. I guess I'm just not that guy."

"I know how you feel," said Monica Chanting's husband Garvin. He was a big guy, built like a brick outhouse. "When I found out about my wife having an affair with Doctor Jones I wanted to squash him like a fly. Stomp on his neck like a viper. Tear him limb from limb like a piñata. Rip him up with my backhoe like a tree stump. Split his head like a melon. But I only found out after he was already dead," he concluded with regret.

All eyes now turned to Jason, who'd gone markedly pale, and was sweating profusely.

"Simply confess, Jason," Omar said kindly. "You'll feel so much better, you'll see."

"But I didn't do it!" Jason cried, his voice shrill. "How can I confess to something I didn't do!"

"So you really want an innocent man to go to prison for a crime you committed?" asked Omar. "You want that on your conscience, too?"

Jason gulped some more.

"He looks guilty, Max," said Dooley.

"He does indeed," I said.

"Think of the twelve steps, son," Father Reilly tried. "Get up and introduce yourself."

Jason stared at the priest, then at the others present, then buried his face in his hands for a moment, before abruptly getting up and saying, in a shaky voice, "My name is Jason and I'm an alcoholic. I'm also... a murderer."

"Why did you do it?" asked Omar, still adopting the same kindly tone he had throughout the meeting.

"I don't know. It came out of nowhere," said Jason, taking a seat again. "I-I'd gone over there to tell him to back off. That I wasn't going to take any more of his crap, and things… got out of hand."

"What crap?" asked Omar.

Jason squeezed his eyes shut, then sighed. "Look, before Jaqlyn joined Soul Science I was the big cheese around here, okay? I was on the inner circle and I was the one sitting next to Master Omar at the table. I was the man, and for the first time ever I felt like my life had purpose, I was going places. People looked up to me and asked me for advice. Girls suddenly started going out with me. Me! Jason Blowhard! It was like a dream."

"And then Jaqlyn showed up," Omar prompted gently.

Jason's expression darkened. "Right from the get-go he started playing mind games. As my doctor he knew all about my past. The boozing, the drugs—"

"Drugs?" asked Odelia, sounding surprised.

"Oh, I've been clean for months," said Jason, like a man at a job interview convincing a future employer of his merits. "But Jaqlyn started telling me it wasn't fitting for an addict to be in my position. He said I was sending out the wrong energetic vibe, and also, I didn't look the part." He touched his face tattoo. "He said I looked like an ex-con and I was liable to scare people away from Soul Science by featuring so prominently in all of the videos. For the sake of the movement he advised me to take a step back and assume a backstage role. At least until I'd had the tattoo removed."

"You never told me this," said Omar.

"I thought you knew!" said Jason. "I thought you knew all, saw all, heard all…"

"Oh, God," said Omar, quite aptly. "I'm just a dude, Jason. All I ever wanted was to bring a little soul into this world. I'm not a god, buddy. Six months ago I was still advising people about Credit Default Swaps and Synthetic Collateralized Debt Obligations! Well, before crashing my Lamborghini Aventador into a guardrail on Route 73, of course."

"Anyway, when I kicked up a fuss about giving up my position on the inner circle and at your table, Jaqlyn said he'd tell everyone about my predilection for hard liquor and coke, and promised I'd be kicked out of Soul Science and lose all my newfound friends."

"My husband was a bastard," said Francine matter-of-factly. "A grade A skunk."

"So I decided to give him a piece of my mind and confront him. I was frankly fed up, and…" He bowed his head. "I kinda lost my nerve and… took a quick snifter."

"Oh, Jason," said Father Reilly.

"It's fine," said Omar. "You fell off the wagon, you can get on again."

"So I accosted Jaqlyn on the street this afternoon and we got into a fight and he said that if I came to his house one more time he was going to make a video and expose me. He'd post it on YouTube and that'd be the end for me. Well, I got very upset and so I grabbed the bottle of vodka I got for the occasion and whacked him on the head with it."

"The devil is in the bottle," Father Reilly murmured, and folded his hands in prayer.

"When he didn't get up, I realized I was in big trouble, but when I looked around I saw that the street was empty. No one had seen us. So I quickly started looking for a car that was unlocked and very soon found one. And then I dumped Jaqlyn's body inside and got the hell out of there."

"Dad left the car unlocked?" asked Odelia, shocked.

Marge closed her eyes and shook her head. "I've only told the man a million times always to lock up his car. But does he do it? No."

"You didn't mean to frame Tex?" asked Uncle Alec.

"I didn't even know whose car it was!" said Jason.

"I think I've heard enough," said Charlene, getting up. "Alec, will you please read Jason his rights?"

Alec did as he was told, and before our very eyes, Jason was arrested and led away.

"I'm sorry, Master Omar!" he said before he was escorted out of the room.

"How did you know?" asked Chase.

Omar emitted a tired sigh. "In Soul Science we have this thing where we write down our thoughts when they're preventing us from getting in touch with our deeper nature. Jason must have come in after what happened this afternoon, and written everything down. I just happened to pass by his desk and saw the notebook. Curious, I took a peek, even though I probably shouldn't have. When I saw what he'd written I immediately thought about calling the cops. Only I realized he'd simply deny the whole thing. So I figured this meeting scenario might induce him to confess. And luckily he did."

"What are you going to do now?" asked Odelia. "Now that you've disbanded Soul Science?"

"Oh, I might take a trip," said Omar. "I made a lot of money in my crazy Wall Street years, and even though I invested a good chunk in Soul Science, I think I want to get away from things for a while. Maybe see my sister. She lives in Spain," he explained.

"You shouldn't give up Soul Science," said Father Reilly now, much to everyone's surprise. "I think you're on to a good thing, Omar, and you shouldn't just give it up. Just... change the format a little bit. I can probably give you some advice on how to do that."

"I would like that," said Omar gratefully.

"Drop by any time. Let's make this work."

People were talking amongst themselves now, discussing the recent and stunning events, and I noticed how Sharif had drifted into my ken and was eyeing me intently.

"Max?" he said now. "We never really had the opportunity to talk, did we?"

"No, we didn't," I said, and didn't mention that I never felt like talking to him.

"The thing is... I think I gave the wrong impression before. Like Omar, I'm just a dude, you know. But you know what cats are like. As soon as you mention the word soul or spirit they immediately assume you're some kind of guru or god or whatever."

"I never thought you were a guru or a god," I said.

"I like your sermons," said Dooley. "I've never slept so well as during the last one. You really should consider putting them on tape and sell them as a patent cure for insomnia."

Sharif, much to my surprise, burst out laughing. "That's the best thing I've heard all week! I'll have to tell Omar."

This intrigued me. "So it's true that Omar can talk to you?"

"Just a figure of speech, Max. He's a human and I'm a cat. Of course we don't talk."

I didn't want to tell him about the Poole women, so I just said, "No, sure, of course."

"Look, Max," he said. "I don't know what's going to happen next. Whether Omar will disband Soul Science or whatever. But I hope you and I can be friends one day."

I looked the cat in the eye, and realized he was just a dude, standing in front of another dude, asking that dude to be his buddy. So I nodded and said, "I'd like that."

"Great," he said, and we shook paws on it.

EPILOGUE

*O*ur company had been requested to liven up yet another garden party, only this party was one conducted in our own backyard, or at least in Marge and Tex's backyard, and only a select few guests were present, namely my humans and my feline friends.

After last night's events had transpired, Tex had immediately been released, and now stood working away behind the grill like a long-lost son finally having arrived home.

If prison life had made him a more spiritual, more reflective person, he didn't show it. As usual he was dispensing the fruits of his labor to all and sundry, regaling both man and beast with pieces of meat like a benevolent King Solomon strewing gold from his hat.

"I think it's wonderful to have Tex home again," said Dooley, who was lying next to me on the porch swing. "The place hasn't been the same without him."

"The place was hardly without him," I pointed out. "He was only in jail a couple of hours."

"Still," said Dooley, directing an affectionate look at our resident doctor-slash-grillmeister.

"Still," I agreed. Tex is one of those people you hardly notice are there, until they're not there and you realize they're actually the bedrock the whole thing is built on.

"I'm very unhappy," Harriet announced. "Shanille played a dirty trick on us."

"Oh, it's all fine, twinkle toes," muttered Brutus, examining a burger patty and, having determined, like the FDA, that it was fit for feline consumption, quickly gobbling it up.

"It's not fine, Brutus. She said she was disbanding cat choir and just when you take your responsibility and step up to the plate, she can't just come in and take over again. She made her bed and now she should lie in it."

"What bed?" asked Dooley.

"Just an expression," I murmured.

"It's all to the good," Brutus insisted.

And he was right. Last night Brutus had conducted his first cat choir ever, and it was safe to say it hadn't gone well. There had been dissent in the ranks, cats had talked through his instructions, and one cat had even thrown a rock at him, like ribald pupils will when they sense the new teacher is a pushover and should be tested to the limit.

I think Brutus learned an important lesson, namely that he isn't a born leader of singers, and that it's a lot tougher than it looks to make a group of unruly cats behave.

So when Shanille suddenly appeared on the scene, a little shamefaced, and asked for a conference with Brutus and myself, I could tell that Brutus was secretly relieved when she apologized for her behavior and asked if she could please take up her old position again.

Brutus immediately said 'Oh, please, yes!' and I agreed it was the best solution for all involved. Shanille, of course, was elated, and kept telling me she had no idea what had come over her, and why she'd fallen under Sharif's spell to such an extent and become absolutely insufferable in the process. I told her not to worry, that we all go off the rails from time to time and that it was all water under the bridge as far as I was concerned.

The only one who wasn't happy was Harriet, and it was obvious that even now, almost a day later, she was still fuming.

"I loved the performance Sharif gave last night," said Dooley now. "He sings better than he preaches. I didn't even fall asleep."

"Yeah, he's got a lovely voice," I agreed.

Sharif, upon his arrival, had been greeted with mixed emotions by his former followers. As soon as he opened his mouth and sang his first song, however, the ice was broken and soon he was accepted by the group as one of the gang. He told us Omar had had his first meeting with Father Reilly, and they'd agreed to work together. Omar would take over the Alcoholics Anonymous group meetings and get busy with some of the other work Father Reilly was involved in. All in all, things were going back to normal.

Even Tex's patients had all returned to the fold. After a little digging, Tex had discovered that Jaqlyn had set up a scam whereby he charged people through the nose for tests they took which were mostly unnecessary. Mrs. Baumgartner's so-called hairline fracture? Non-existent. Just a way for Jaqlyn to make more money, in cahoots with a shady lab technician and a crooked radiologist, who provided the bogus tests. After Odelia had revealed all, Tex had suddenly been overwhelmed by an outpouring of sympathy. Being the man that he was, though, he'd adopted a forgive and forget attitude.

"You know, I think we all learned an important lesson," said Gran.

"And what lesson is that?" asked Odelia.

"That anyone can be a religious leader," said Gran.

"Is that the lesson you learned?" asked Chase. "I learned another one. That I should never arrest a member of my family again, no matter what the law advises."

"Oh, don't be too hard on yourself, Chase," said Tex, gleefully flinging a burger patty into Marcie and Ted Trapper's backyard. "I don't blame you for arresting me. In fact I can't think of a better person to arrest me than you. I even enjoyed our interview."

Chase winced. "I'm sorry, Tex. I really thought you lost your head and killed the guy."

"Hey, no hard feelings," Tex insisted.

"Want some more potato salad, Alec?" asked Marge.

"Don't mind if I do, Marge," said Alec, perking up.

"Then get it yourself," said Marge harshly, and snatched the bowl away.

"Looks like Marge still hasn't forgiven her brother," said Dooley.

"No, looks like," I agreed.

"Don't be this way, Marge," said Uncle Alec. "I was only doing my duty."

"The only reason you were invited is because Ma told me I should," Marge snapped. "So if you don't want me to change my mind and kick you out, I suggest you shut up."

"Ouch," said Brutus.

"Ouch indeed," I said.

"It's all fine," said Tex, lovingly setting a plate of scorched sausages on the table for everyone to enjoy. "We're all friends here. Forgive and forget, eh?"

"Mh," said Marge, not convinced.

"So how is the article coming along?" asked Chase, deciding to change the subject.

"It's a little challenging," Odelia said. "I wrote one on the rise and fall of Soul Science, and one on the rise and fall of Jaqlyn, but Dan told me I should probably write another one on the rise and fall and rise again of Dad, as people loved the last one. And now we don't know which one to print, as we only have so much space on our front page."

"I think I'll launch my own religion," Gran announced suddenly. "I've seen how it's done now, and I think I would like the perks of having my own set of loyal followers."

"The only thing you'd like is for Scarlett to sit at your feet in worship," said Marge.

Gran's wide grin said it all. "And would that be such a bad thing?"

"Don't do it, Ma," Uncle Alec warned.

"Yeah, don't even think about it," Marge said.

"But it's so easy! And look how much money you can make. We could do it as a family. Tex could retire, and so could Alec and Marge. Chase could work security at events, Marge could be my communications director, Odelia could write my press releases, and Tex and Alec could bring in the followers. It'll be a goldmine for the whole family!"

"Ma, no!" said Alec and Marge as one voice. They shared a look and grinned.

"I'm sorry, big brother," said Marge.

"No, I'm sorry, little sis," said Alec.

And as brother and sister hugged it out, I could see Gran direct a sly look at her offspring. When she caught my eye, she winked.

"She did it on purpose," I muttered.

"What's that?" asked Dooley.

"Nothing, Dooley. Just that Gran isn't half as crazy as she looks."

I saw that she was studying Chase next, clearly wondering how to raise the cop's stock in Marge's eyes. I could practically see her little gray cells work like little beavers underneath those little white curls of hers.

"You know?" she said, sidling up to Marge and lowering her voice. "I'm glad you finally see Chase for what he is: a traitorous, no-good piece of cheese. So I was thinking. We need to find a new boyfriend for Odelia and get rid of this Chase Kingsley once and for all. So how about Barney Sowman? He's single, right?" Marge gave her mother a shocked look, and opened her mouth to speak, but before she could, Gran went on, "Or how about Omar Carter? You heard what he said. The guy is loaded. A great catch."

Marge's lips had formed a thin line, and her face had turned into a thunderstorm.

She got up slowly and said, eyes popping a little, "Vesta Muffin, if you think for one minute I'm going to allow my daughter to break up with the best man she's ever met you've got another thing coming! Chase is a part of this family and he's here to stay!"

"Fine," said Gran, crossing her arms with a mutinous look on her face. "If you want to keep nourishing a viper in your bosom, it's your funeral. I'm just saying Omar is—"

"Not another word from you!" Marge thundered.

Gran shrugged, and when I met her eye, this time I was the one who winked.

Yep. One smart cookie, our Grandma Muffin.

"C'mere, Chase," said Marge, her voice tremulous, and enveloped the cop into a warm embrace. "I'm sorry," she said, blinking away a tear.

"No, I'm sorry, Marge," said Chase, his eyes moist.

"You're like a son to me, you know that, right?"

"And you're like a mother to me," he said.

"Let me get in there," said Tex, and joined the hugfest, quickly followed by Uncle Alec.

"Max?" asked Dooley.

"Mh?" I said, enjoying the scene and swiping at my eyes.

"How can Marge be like a mother to Chase if he already has a mother?"

"I have no idea, buddy, but isn't it wonderful, everyone getting along?"

Brutus and Harriet had slunk off the swing and were traipsing up to the grill, presumably to see if more meat was to be had. Harriet was still complaining about Shanille, and Brutus was still dutifully nodding along, not all that concerned.

"Max?"

"Mh?"

"If Marge is like a dad to Chase, is Tex like a father?"

"I guess so," I said.

"But… then isn't Odelia like a sister to him?"

"Um…"

"Brothers and sisters can't get married, Max. I saw that on TV. They just can't."

I patted him on the head. "You know what, Dooley? You think too much."

"But—"

"It's all to the good, buddy. Just relax and be happy."

He heaved a deep sigh. "Okay," he said, and to my surprise gave me a grateful smile.

"What?" I said.

"You said I think too much."

"So?"

"That means I'm smart, right?"

"Of course you're smart."

His smile widened. "No one has ever told me I'm smart, Max."

"Well, you are, Dooley, and don't let anyone tell you different."

To my surprise he suddenly gave me a big hug. "I love you, Max."

"I love you, too, buddy."

Yep. It was a real lovefest.

And you know what?

I loved every second.

Guess I'm a softie, too.

EXCERPT FROM DEATH IN SUBURBIA (THE KELLYS BOOK 2)

Chapter One

"Scott! Get up! Time for breakfast!"

Scott groaned, opened one eye and saw that the day had already started without him. He didn't mind. As far as he was concerned, the day could do whatever it wanted. So he closed his eyes again and tried to return to the dream he'd abandoned. The one where he was Han Solo and instead of having to endure that weird hairy ape as a traveling companion he conquered the universe with Emilia Clarke by his side. Now wouldn't *that* be something!

But before he and lovely Emilia could board the Millennium Falcon, Mom's voice pierced the fragile fabric of sleep once more—effectively ending his roseate dreamscape.

"Scott! Out of bed! Now!"

He threw back the comforter, rubbed the sleep from his eyes and yawned. Checking his smartphone, he saw that his best friend Mike was still asleep. If he wasn't he'd have sent him an update on his Pokemon Go conquests from last night. They might be twelve, but that didn't mean Pokemon was beneath them now. Besides, with the new Harry Potter Pokemon coming out soon, they needed to work on their mad skillz.

Shuffling out of his room in the direction of the bathroom, he discovered the door locked. Dragging one hand through his shaggy mane, he pounded the door with the other.

"Go away, scuzz-ball!" his sister yelled from inside.

"You go away, snarf-face!" he yelled back.

"Don't call your sister a snarf-face," said his mother as she hurried past, cradling the baby in her arms.

"Why do you keep carrying Jacob everywhere?" he asked. "He's old enough to walk."

But Mom wasn't listening. Instead, she was pounding down the stairs, still carrying Jacob as if his legs were too weak to carry him. At this rate, the toddler was never going to learn how to walk all by himself. Scott shook his head. Adults. They just never listened.

The door to the bathroom suddenly swung open and Maya appeared, a towel draped around her head and another one around her bony frame. She narrowed her eyes at him. "Why do you need the bathroom anyway? You wear the same grungy shirt three days in a row and you don't even bother to deodorize those pathetic pits of yours."

"I don't need to deodorize my pits," he said, moving past his sister. "My pits naturally smell like roses."

"Nobody's pits smell like roses. Especially yours, little brother."

He squared off against Maya. Even though she was five years older than him, they were the same height. He'd gotten a growth spurt last year to the extent she had no right to call him 'little brother' anymore. "Are you dissing my pits?"

"I'm telling you that if you don't start working on your

personal hygiene no girl is ever going to want to go out with you."

He laughed at this. "Who cares about girls?! All girls are stupid!"

"Have it your own way, freak. I'm just trying to look out for you."

She stomped off, and he plodded into the bathroom and slammed the door.

Dee heard the door slam and yelled, "Don't slam the door!"

Not that it would do much good. Her kids were at the stage where they'd stopped listening to anything she or Tom said. She remembered just in time not to frown. She was turning forty next year, and she could almost feel the collagen in her face breaking down as that fateful birthday drew closer. Likewise, she tried not to smile too much either, or pucker her lips. She darted a quick look in the hallway mirror. The woman who looked back at her was fair-haired, light-skinned, and quite beautiful. She also had dark rings under her eyes that hadn't been there when she was her lookalike daughter's age. Ugh.

Inadvertently, she'd put Jacob down. The toddler was looking up at her, then gave her a cheerful smile. "Mommy!" he cried, then held out his arms. "Carry!"

Scott's words hadn't missed their effect, though. Her son was right. The days of lugging the little tyke all over the place were over. In Dee's defense, though, she only carried him up and down the stairs these days, and only when she was in a hurry. "Go to the kitchen," she said encouragingly. "Go and find Daddy."

"Daddy!" Jacob said, and lo and behold, he moved off at an awkward wobble in the general direction of the kitchen.

As she followed him at a little distance, Dee smiled. He was such a lively, cheerful little dude. Never gave his mom and dad any trouble at all. Unlike Scott, who'd been a real cryer, and Maya, who'd been a restless kid. Looked like third time was the charm after all.

Behind her, Ralph came trotting down the stairs, his nails clicking funnily on the steps. The family Goldendoodle was a late riser, too, and proved it by plopping down on his heinie and yawning widely. He then barked once and followed Dee into the kitchen, where he proceeded to hover over his food bowl and give it a tentative sniff before digging in.

Meanwhile Dee's husband of twenty years, Tom Kelly, was juggling a skillet and a glass bowl of pancake batter, creating the perfect morning treat. A pot of coffee stood spreading its wonderful aroma through the kitchen and the table was already set for six. Dee's mom Caroline was presiding over the breakfast nook, preparing the kids' lunches.

"Mom," said Dee as she hoisted Jacob into his seat, "I told you. Maya doesn't need you to pack her a school lunch. She grabs whatever from the cafeteria." Or the Starbucks around the corner.

"I don't mind," said Mom as she added an apple to the lunch box. "Besides, the stuff they offer at schools these days is not healthy. Just a steaming pile of junk food. Unfit for man or beast."

"They have a healthy alternative," she said as she outfitted her youngest with a bib.

"You know kids. When they have a choice between a greasy burger or a plate of veggies they'll take the burger every time. Honestly, Dee, how hard is it to prepare a healthy and nutritious lunch?"

"Not hard at all. Problem is she won't eat it. I can tell you that right now. She'll dump it in the trash first chance she gets."

"No, she won't. Not when her grammy put that extra-special ingredient in there. Love," she explained.

"Love or no love—she'll trash it. Just you wait and see."

Dee's mom stubbornly pursed her lips. "No, she won't. My angel wouldn't do that to a lunch her own grammy packed. Nuh-uh."

Dee wanted to explain that Maya had stopped being an angel a long time ago but decided this was a battle she was never going to win.

"Honey," said her husband, setting down a plate of pancakes. "Can you try one? I have a feeling I forgot to add something but I don't know what it is."

Dee forked a pancake and took a bite. She grimaced. "You forgot the sugar, hon."

"Dang it," Tom murmured. "Knew I'd left something out."

Dee shared a smile with her mother. Tom really was the absent-minded professor incarnate. Not only was he a real-life professor—in economics, not chemistry—but he was as scatterbrained as they came.

"Don't you worry about a thing, Tom," said Mom. "We'll just add more jam." And to show them she meant business, she spooned a generous helping of strawberry jam onto her pancake and transferred it into her mouth. Talk about your healthy alternative.

"Kids!" Tom bellowed at the foot of the stairs. "If you don't get down here right now we're all gonna be late for school!" He darted a quick look at his wife. "And the gallery!"

"I don't know why you keep going to that place," said Mom as she added a granola bar to Scott's lunchbox. "You hired that nice girl—what's-her-name—I wanna say Trixie?"

"Holly," Dee corrected her mother, then tucked a small piece of apple into Jacob's mouth. He happily munched down on it, half the apple soon dribbling down his chin. "And the reason I keep going is because it's my gallery, Mom. I'm the one in charge."

"Sounds to me like this Trixie person is on top of things."

"Holly. And she is on top of things. But I still have to be there to handle stuff like acquisitions, communicating with the artists and collectors, setting up exhibitions…"

Mom was waving her hand. "Trixie can handle all of that stuff." She gestured to Jacob. "What she can't do is take care of your baby. That is something only you can do. Raising your kid. A few short years from now all three of your babies will be gone and that gallery will still be there waiting for you to run it. Not that I mind babysitting my grandchild," she quickly added when Dee opened her mouth to respond. "In fact I love it. But a mother leaving her child at home all day?" She shrugged. "It's just not right."

"Do you think I want to be in Seattle when I could be here at home with Jacob?"

"Oh, I know, sweetie," said her mother, reaching over to pinch her cheek as if she was the toddler, not Jacob. "But actions speak louder than words, so get your priorities straight, all right? And I'm sure Tom will back me up on this —won't you, Tom?"

Tom looked up from his study of the bowl of leftover pancake batter, a confused look on his face. At forty-eight, he actually managed to look younger than his wife, who was almost a decade his junior. How he did this, Dee did not know. "Mh?" said Tom.

"Do you or don't you agree that your wife should be home with her child instead of gallivanting around with a bunch of wannabe artists?" said Mom, enunciating clearly and distinctly as if addressing a three-year-old.

Tom's eyes shifted to Dee. "Um…"

"Oh, for crying out loud," Mom said, throwing up her hands.

"You know, if you want to stay home I'm sure we can arrange something," said Tom. "I mean financially we can definitely manage, so…"

"Look, I love my job, all right? I worked hard to set up that gallery and I can't afford to abandon it when it's still finding its feet. People who visit the Dee Kelly Gallery expect to find Dee Kelly there to greet them, not a salaried second-in-command. Besides, I'm just working mornings right now."

"You're absolutely right," said Tom soothingly, then moved over to peck a quick kiss to her brow.

"Looks like we've been vetoed, little man," said Mom, tucking a piece of pancake into Jacob's mouth.

The toddler happily gobbled up the treat, then cackled loudly. "Want more!" he yelled.

"Looks like we're getting new neighbors," said Scott, slouching into the kitchen, then draping his limp frame across a chair as if he were a bag of bones instead of a real boy.

"New neighbors?" asked Tom. "What do you mean?"

"I mean there's a moving truck backing up the driveway as we speak."

All eyes moved to the window, which offered a great view of the house next door. Scott was right. A truck was backing up the neighboring driveway, two burly movers instructing the driver with word and gesture.

"Huh," said Tom. "I didn't even know the house had been sold."

Maya waltzed into the kitchen, her eyes glued to her smartphone. "You guys, did you know that Gwen Stefani is having another baby? Isn't she, like, a thousand years old or something?"

Tom looked offended. "Gwen Stefani is my age," he said.

"Yeah, well, newsflash, Dad," said Maya. "You're old, too."

"We're getting new neighbors," Scott announced. "I hope they have a dog."

Maya's eyes snapped to the window. "Neighbors?" When she noticed the moving van, her jaw fell. "Are you kidding me right now?" She turned to her mother. "Mom—I told you we should have gotten those curtains up. Now what am I going to do?"

Scott grinned. "Relax, fuzz-face. Nobody's gonna look through your window."

"Shut up. Mom! I need curtains ASAP!"

"A girl needs her privacy," Dee's mom agreed.

"Dad!" Maya cried plaintively. "I can't have a bunch of hormonal teenagers spying on me!"

"You won't, darling," said Tom. "I'll get you those curtains. And you, Scott."

"I don't need no curtains," said Scott, shoving his fifth pancake into his mouth, this one drowning in syrup. "Unlike my sister, I got nothing to hide." Even with his mouth full of pancake, he managed a smirk, earning him a vicious scowl from Maya.

Dee's eyes happened to wander over to the clock on the kitchen wall. When she saw what time it was, she jolted into action. "You guys, we have to get moving. Scott—thank your grandmother for preparing your lunch—you, too, Maya. Chop, chop! Let's go, Kellys!"

Within five minutes, they were all racing for the exit, Dee after giving Baby Jacob a smacking kiss on the sticky cheek and promising her mother she'd be home in a couple of hours. And then they were off, leaving the kitchen a mess and Caroline shaking her head at the hullabaloo a family of five could create.

Dee then stuck her head back in. "Love you, Mom," she said. "Wouldn't know what to do without you."

"Get out of here, you," said Caroline. Then, when Dee directed a dazzling smile at her, added grudgingly, "I love you, too. Now better get going, or Trixie will be pissed."

Chapter Two

Scott took his bike from the garage and waved to Mike, who was staring at the moving van.

"Hey, buddy," said Scott as he rode up to his friend.

"You're getting new neighbors," Mike said, showing his keen powers of observation.

"Yeah. I hope they've got a dog."

"A dog? A girl, you mean."

"Girl? What girl?"

"A girl our age! A girl you can fall in love with—moon over while you're staring out of your window while she's staring out of hers." He'd pressed his hands to his chest and was looking up at the sky. "A girl so pretty you'll write her *poems* and sing her songs of *love*."

Scott eyed his friend with an expression of abject horror on his freckled face. "Are you crazy? Who needs girls?!"

"We do," said Mike as he craned his neck to catch a glimpse of whoever was moving in next door.

It shouldn't have surprised Scott that his friend felt this way. Mike was something of a dork. With his braces and his glasses he looked like one, too. Not that it bothered Scott. Mike had been his buddy ever since the Kellys moved from Medina to Issaquah where they now lived. Changing neighborhoods had been tough, but not as tough as changing schools. Making new friends had been an iffy proposition at first, and it was only when he and Mike had bonded over their shared ability to squirt orange juice out of their noses that things had started looking up again. Now they were inseparable.

"I like girls," Mike said reverently. "I like Maggie Cooper."

"Who's Maggie Cooper?"

"She's only the prettiest girl in school. Hair like spun gold. Eyes like Alaskan lakes. A nose like..." He frowned, his poetic prowess momentarily deserting him. "A nose like, um..."

"Yeah, yeah. I get the picture," said Scott, who, unlike Mike, didn't worship at the feet of girls—even if their hair was like spun gold—whatever spun gold was. "Let's get going, buddy. We're gonna be late."

As they rode off on their bikes, the two friends briefly looked back, Mike to see if his friend had just acquired a girl-next-door who could melt his barnacled heart, and Scott to try and catch a glimpse of the dog he hoped these mysterious new neighbors had brought.

Maya's boyfriend was already sitting in his Ford Mustang, parked at the curb, the motor rumbling impressively. The car was a junker Mark's dad had gotten him for his sixteenth birthday but it still worked fine enough. Mark had painted it bright orange with pink stripes in deference to Maya, knowing they were her favorite colors. Maya owned her own car, a pink Mini Cooper, but Mark refused to be seen dead in the thing. Apart from that minor character flaw, the stocky Mark Dean, self-proclaimed football jock, was a surprisingly kind-hearted soul. And as the son of a lumber mill tycoon, he was also comfortably well-off. Not that that mattered a great deal to Maya, whose dad wasn't exactly a pauper either.

"You've got new neighbors," said Mark as Maya slid into the seat.

"Yeah—I hope they're nice. Not like the ones we had in Medina."

The house where they'd lived had been partially blown up

in a home invasion gone wrong. Luckily the Kelly clan had escaped the ordeal unscathed, but they'd still opted to sell the house and relocate to a part of town that wouldn't be a constant reminder of that fateful night.

"Those home invaders weren't neighbors, though, right?"

"Not technically," she admitted. The leader of the gang had been a Seattle mobster. Not a neighbor, per se, but close enough. "Let's not talk about that, Mark."

He gave her a rueful look. "I'm sorry. I won't mention it again."

Strictly speaking, she'd been the one to dredge up the wretched past, but watching Mark's expression of contrition was too much fun. She placed a hand on his cheek. "That's all right, Mark. You can always make it up to me."

His face lit up with a goofy grin. "That's more like it. Anything you want, babe."

She grimaced. "First off, don't call me babe. I hate it. Second, you can start by driving me to school. We're going to be late."

"What happened to your car?"

"Being serviced. Engine trouble." In actual fact she'd scratched the paint by hitting the mailbox last night, but she wasn't going to give Mark a reason to mock her driving skills.

Dad had bought her the car because school was now a respectable distance from her house, owing to the fact that she'd opted to stay in the same school as before, when they were still living in Medina. Seeing as she only had one more year of high school to go, it would have been a shame to switch schools like her little brother had done. One more year and she was off to college—the same university where her dad taught: the University of Washington, also known as U-Dub.

"So have you thought about filling out that college application?" she asked Mark as he eased the car away from the curb.

"Um…"

She rolled her eyes. "Mark! You promised!"

"The thing is… my dad keeps talking retirement. I don't want to let the old man down."

"Your dad has been talking retirement since he took over from his dad." She tucked a lock of blond hair behind her ear. "You know you'll be able to take that company and launch it into the stratosphere if you get an economics degree, right? My dad explained all that to you."

"I know, babe. It's just that… my grades just aren't that great."

She knew what he meant. Mark was a sweetheart, and a great athlete. What he wasn't was academically gifted. "I'm sure with a little help from me and my dad you'll do just fine. Remember, you don't have to graduate at the top of your class, Mark. You just have to graduate, period."

He emitted a noncommittal sound, then focused on the road. She gritted her teeth in disappointment. He was going to take his dad's advice and take over the lumber mill, wasn't he? Who needs a college education when you've got a perfectly good job waiting for you? And his dad had been talking retirement mainly because the Seattle weather was wreaking havoc on his arthritic joints and he was dreaming of becoming a snowbird.

What she didn't want to admit was the real reason she wanted Mark to join her at UW: the fact that she feared drifting apart if he were to join his family company while she became a college student. She punched his shoulder.

"Ow! What did you do that for?" he said.

She punched his shoulder again, harder this time.

"Hey! That's my good arm. I need that arm."

She gave him another few light punches.

"You punch like a girl," he chuckled.

"That's probably because I am a girl."

He gave her a quick sideways glance. "Are you all right?"

She did the eye roll thing again. "What do you think?"

He narrowed his eyes. "Is it that time of the month again?"

She raised her fist to give him her biggest punch yet but by now he was laughing so hard she decided not to bother. "You know what, Mark? If you don't want to go to college with me just say so. Don't give me this lame excuse of your dad says this and your dad says that."

"But my dad really says all those things!"

"Ugh," she said, and settled down in her seat, her arms folded across her chest.

"I want to go to college with you, babe," he said finally. "It's just that… I don't think I'm smart enough, okay?"

She looked up, surprised. "What are you talking about?"

"Your dad—he's like, a genius, okay? But every time he talks shop, my eyes glaze over. I don't understand a word he's saying! So I figure four years of that is going to kill me—if I ever make it that far in the first place. I'm not college material, babe—I'm just not!"

She was touched by the vulnerability he displayed. It was a side of him he rarely showed. "I'm sure that with a little tutoring from my dad—"

"But that's just it. I listen to the guy and I blank out. Completely! It's like listening to Coach Martin when he's trying to introduce a new running play. I'm not smart that way. I need to see something with my own eyes—go through the motions a couple times before I get it. And this economics gobbledygook is just… gobbledygook!"

She grinned. She got it now, and patted him on the shoulder. "Don't you worry about a thing. Just follow my lead and you'll make it through four years of gobbledygook just fine."

Now that she knew what ailed him, she knew exactly what to do about it, too.

He gave her a curious glance. "Uh-oh," he said. "I know that look."

"What look?"

"You've got some kind of plan, don't you?"

"Of course I've got a plan. Never go through life without a plan. Isn't that what I keep telling you?"

He gave her a lost-puppy look. "Uh-huh," he said tentatively.

She patted his shoulder again. "I've got this," she assured him.

"That's what I'm afraid of," he murmured.

Chapter Three

As Tom drove the family Toyota Sienna out of the driveway he stared so hard at the moving van he almost clipped the mailbox.

"Watch out!" Dee cried.

He stomped on the brake and the car screeched to a standstill. "I wonder who they are," he said as he eased the car into reverse and backed up. "First thing tonight let's go over and introduce ourselves." Already he was painting a mental picture of their new neighbor. A professor, just like himself—possibly in a less technical field. Archeology? Or something really cool like robotics or artificial intelligence? They could chat over the hedge—exchange ideas while their wives socialized over preprandial martinis on the patio. Or he could show his new neighbor his newly acquired collection of model trains and tracks.

In his mind's eye he was already picturing himself and this kindly man who was a few years his senior rolling up their collective sleeves and constructing a train track in their combined backyards, just like Walt Disney did back in the day. Wouldn't that be something?

"Do you want me to drive, honey?" asked his wife, giving him a worried look.

"Mh? Oh, no, I'm fine. Just wondering… Do people still bring over a freshly baked pie? Or is that too old-fashioned?"

"We can bring a pie," said Dee. "Or a bottle of wine. Just not sure if they're…"

"The pie-eating or the wine-drinking kind of people," Tom finished the sentence. "Gotcha. Probably we should—"

"—spy out who they are before we commit ourselves to one or the other."

Now they were both staring, as Tom drove the car at a snail's pace past the neighboring house.

"I don't see anyone," said Tom. "Maybe they sent the movers ahead of them."

"Or maybe it's Brad Pitt and he'll move in under the cloak of darkness and we'll never get to see him as he'll be coming and going through a secret passageway in the basement."

Tom gave his wife a curious look. "Brad Pitt? Really?"

"I wouldn't mind if Angelina Jolie moved in so you can't mind if Brad Pitt moves in."

"You do know that Brangelina is no more, right?"

"Of course I know. Brad is single now," she said with a touch of wistfulness.

They stared some more. "I just hope they're nice people," said Tom. With a keen interest in model trains who didn't mind getting their hands dirty while laying track.

"And I hope they have a boy Scott's age and a girl Maya's age and the kids can bond."

"Don't forget a dog who's Ralph's age and a baby Jacob's age."

He touched his foot down on the accelerator and soon they were cruising through the neighborhood, which consisted entirely of similar houses to their own. After last year's home invasion, the Kelly family mantra was not to stand out, and stand out they definitely did not. They drove a nice sensible family car, occupied a nice sensible single-family home, and lived a nice sensible family life. Nothing to see here, folks. Move right along!

❧

After he'd dropped off his wife at the art gallery, Tom proceeded towards his own place of business, the university he called his home away from home. Breezing into his office, he plunked down his floppy brown leather satchel, drew a hand through his floppy brown hair and dropped down in his swivel chair, booting up his computer as he did. Before he had a chance to check his schedule, a knock on the door alerted him of his first visitor.

"Come in!" he boomed.

The door opened and a head poked in. The head was pale and festooned with red spots, the few remaining hairs on the top awkwardly combed to cover the acreage.

"Hey, Tom," said Elliott Lusky, head of the history department.

"Elliott," said Tom jovially. "So have you thought about my offer?"

Elliott shook his bulbous head mournfully. "No can do, I'm afraid. The wife has been nagging me to take her on one of those Alaskan cruises and she's earmarked every last penny in our savings account for that particular purpose. Terribly inconvenient, I know."

Tom leaned back in his chair. "Can't you tell her you're allergic to Alaska or something?" Ever since Tom had seen a documentary about Walt Disney's love for model trains he'd been dreaming of building his own, smaller version of the impressive set Uncle Walt had built in his backyard in the fifties. To this end he needed allies—friends he could share his new passion with. And Elliott was just such a friend. Unfortunately the tubby little man was displaying an awful lot of sales resistance.

"I'm afraid not," said Elliott with a look of apology on his face. "She wanted to go last year. I managed to stave off the disaster by claiming Alaska was in fact part of Canada and we'd need a visa, which we'd never get as I've been declared persona non grata in Canuck country ever since I got drunk and disorderly on a high school trip to Montreal."

"You don't need a visa to visit Canada."

"I know that. The point is that Esther doesn't—or didn't." He frowned. "Curse the internet. Not only does she know I lied to her about Alaska being a part of Canada, she's starting to suspect I made up that whole thing about being arrested in Montreal."

"Were you ever arrested in Montreal?"

Tom's colleague rearranged his features into an appropriate expression of contrition. "No, I was not. An exceedingly nice police officer once cautioned me for jaywalking, though."

"I don't think that counts."

"I don't think so either. Anyway, as it stands she's already booked the tickets so it looks like I'm in for it. I'll have to traipse along while she watches humpback whales cavort in the surf or glides down one of those wretched glaciers."

"Do people actually glide down glaciers? I would have thought that was dangerous. People have been known to tumble down a crevasse never to be seen again."

A gleam of hope lit up the distinguished history professor's face. But then he shook his head, the gleam extinguished. "With my luck that will never happen." He checked his watch. "Have to run, Tom. I've got a class to teach on the

Borgia family." He stared before him for a moment. "They were very fond of arsenic, those Borgias. Liked to poison their husbands. And their wives. Excruciatingly painful, death by arsenic. Very effective."

And with these words he held up his hand and withdrew, gently closing the door.

ABOUT NIC

Nic Saint is the pen name for writing couple Nick and Nicole Saint. They've penned novels in the romance, cat sleuth, middle grade, suspense, comedy and cozy mystery genres. Nicole has a background in accounting and Nick in political science and before being struck by the writing bug the Saints worked odd jobs around the world (including massage therapist in Mexico, gardener in Italy, restaurant manager in India, and Berlitz teacher in Belgium).

When they're not writing they enjoy Christmas-themed Hallmark movies (whether it's Christmas or not), all manner of pastry, comic books, a daily dose of yoga (to limber up those limbs), and spoiling their big red tomcat Tommy.

www.nicsaint.com

ALSO BY NIC SAINT

The Mysteries of Max

Purrfect Murder

Purrfectly Deadly

Purrfect Revenge

Purrfect Heat

Purrfect Crime

Purrfect Rivalry

Purrfect Peril

Purrfect Secret

Purrfect Alibi

Purrfect Obsession

Purrfect Betrayal

Purrfectly Clueless

Purrfectly Royal

Purrfect Cut

Purrfect Trap

Purrfectly Hidden

Purrfect Kill

Purrfect Boy Toy

Purrfectly Dogged

Purrfectly Dead

Purrfect Saint

Box Set 1 (Books 1-3)

Box Set 2 (Books 4-6)

Box Set 3 (Books 7-9)
Box Set 4 (Books 10-12)
Box Set 5 (Books 13-15)
Box Set 6 (Books 16-18)

Purrfect Santa
Purrfectly Flealess

Nora Steel
Murder Retreat

The Kellys
Murder Motel
Death in Suburbia

Emily Stone
Murder at the Art Class

Washington & Jefferson
First Shot

Alice Whitehouse
Spooky Times
Spooky Trills
Spooky End
Spooky Spells

Ghosts of London
Between a Ghost and a Spooky Place
Public Ghost Number One
Ghost Save the Queen

Box Set 1 (Books 1-3)

A Tale of Two Harrys

Ghost of Girlband Past

Ghostlier Things

Charleneland

Deadly Ride

Final Ride

Neighborhood Witch Committee

Witchy Start

Witchy Worries

Witchy Wishes

Saffron Diffley

Crime and Retribution

Vice and Verdict

Felonies and Penalties (Saffron Diffley Short 1)

The B-Team

Once Upon a Spy

Tate-à-Tate

Enemy of the Tates

Ghosts vs. Spies

The Ghost Who Came in from the Cold

Witchy Fingers

Witchy Trouble

Witchy Hexations

Witchy Possessions

Witchy Riches

Box Set 1 (Books 1-4)

The Mysteries of Bell & Whitehouse

One Spoonful of Trouble

Two Scoops of Murder

Three Shots of Disaster

Box Set 1 (Books 1-3)

A Twist of Wraith

A Touch of Ghost

A Clash of Spooks

Box Set 2 (Books 4-6)

The Stuffing of Nightmares

A Breath of Dead Air

An Act of Hodd

Box Set 3 (Books 7-9)

A Game of Dons

Standalone Novels

When in Bruges

The Whiskered Spy

ThrillFix

Homejacking

The Eighth Billionaire

The Wrong Woman

Made in the USA
Columbia, SC
01 July 2020